Published in Moonstone
by Rupa Publications India Pvt. Ltd 2025
7/16, Ansari Road, Daryaganj
New Delhi 110002

Sales centres:
Bengaluru Chennai
Hyderabad Jaipur Kathmandu
Kolkata Mumbai Prayagraj

P-ISBN: 978-93-6156-539-7
E-ISBN: 978-93-6156-555-7

First impression 2025

10 9 8 7 6 5 4 3 2 1

Printed in India

Contents

Armoured Dinosaurs

Ceratop Dinosaurs

Cretaceous Dinosaurs

Flying Dinosaurs

Jurassic Dinosaurs

Ornithopod Dinosaurs

Sauropod Dinosaurs

Sea Dinosaurs

Theropods Dinosaurs

Triassic Dinosaurs

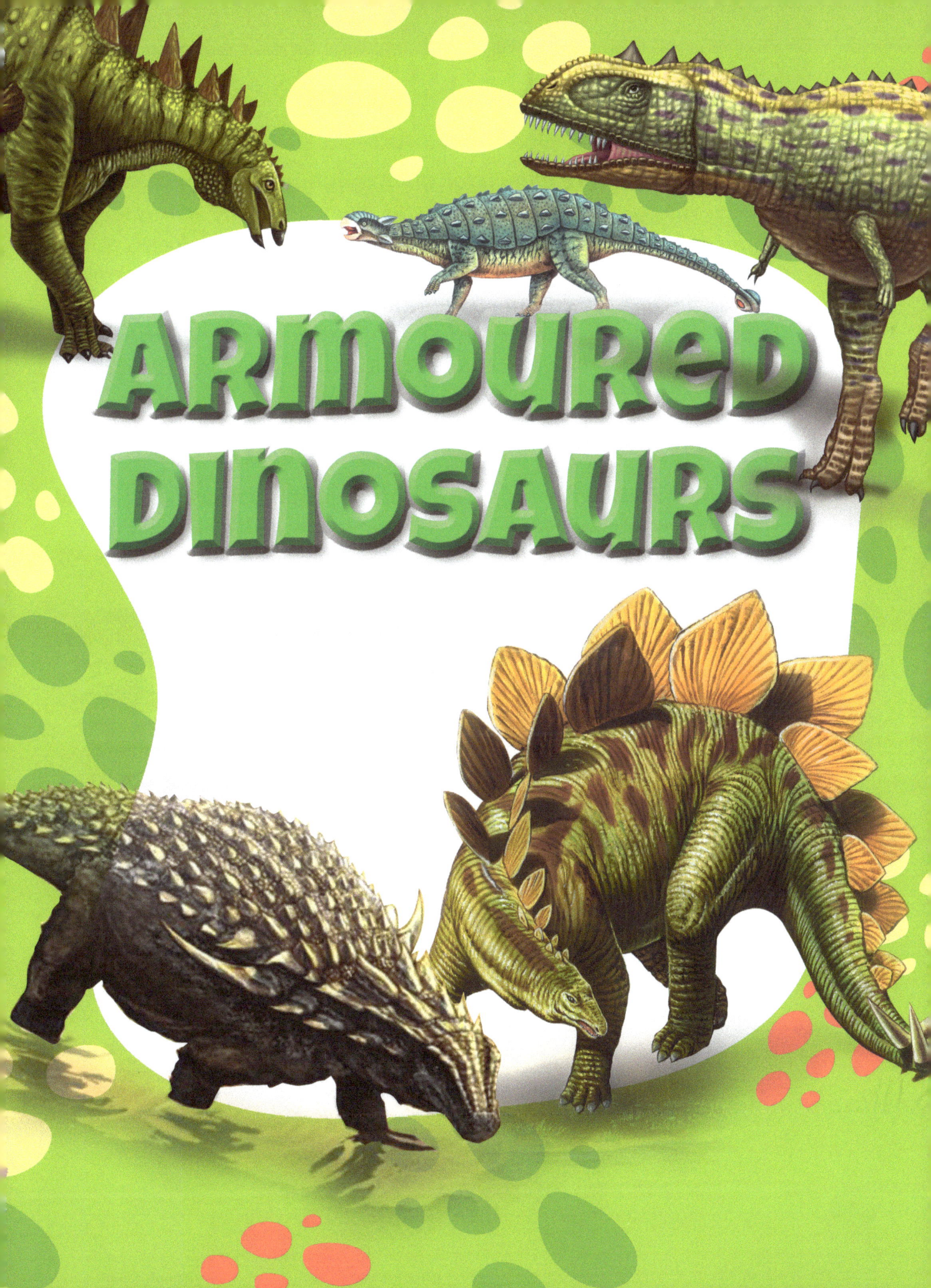

ARMOURED DINOSAURS

Armoured
Dinosaurs

Armoured dinosaurs were known for their combinations of plates and spikes all over the back, body, tail and head. They had bony scutes which were similar to the modern day crocodiles, which later took forms that were more complex like large plates, clubs and carapaces. Their heavy armour was an anti-predation strategy and these dinosaurs evolved only during the Early Jurassic period and continued to stay till the Late Cretaceous period.

Ankylosaurs

The Ankylosaurs first appeared during the Late Cretaceous period and were renowned for their heavy armour. Their name, meaning "Fused Lizard," refers to their rigid, bony plates. Weighing approximately six tonnes, these herbivores grazed on ferns and low-lying vegetation. Measuring around 10 metres in length, they were often called "living tanks" due to their heavily spiked armour. At the end of their tails, they had a rounded club, which they used as a formidable weapon against predators. Despite their strength, Ankylosaurs were slow-moving animals, only slightly faster than a turtle.

Edmontonia

The Edmontonias were built to stand their ground and fight, unlike many other armoured dinosaurs. Although they were easy prey for a large, hungry Tyrannosaurus rex, they could still defend themselves against other predators. These herbivores walked on all fours, relying on their spines and large spikes along their sides to appear more formidable to attackers. Their tails were similar to sharp, bony whips, which may have been effective in slashing at a tyrannosaur's legs during combat.

Ankylosaurus

Euoplocephalus

The Euoplocephalus were among the most common dinosaurs of the Late Cretaceous period. Even their eyelids had spikes to protect their eyes. They had spikes and bony protrusions along the sides of their heads, extending down their armoured backs. Their tails ended with a hammer-like club, which they used to fend off large Theropod predators. Weighing around four tonnes, they were strict herbivores.

Shamosaurus

The Shamosauruses were herbivorous, basal Ankylosaurians with evenly spaced spiked projections along their backs. They were among the first armoured dinosaurs to evolve a clubbed tail. They lived during the Early Cretaceous period and were notable for their robust skull structures. Their teeth were adapted for consuming soft vegetation.

Nodosaurus

The name Nodosaurus, meaning "knobbed lizard," refers to an early nodosaurid dinosaur known for its exceptional fossil preservation. This armoured plant-eater belonged to the nodosaurid family, a subgroup of ankylosaurs. It measured between 13 and 20 feet in length and weighed approximately one tonne. Unlike later ankylosaurs, it lacked a tail club but relied on its bony armour for defence.

Euoplocephalus

Jurassic
Armoured Dinosaurs

The first armoured dinosaurs emerged in the Early Jurassic period, following the mass extinction event at the end of the Triassic. These dinosaurs were among the earliest to develop bony protection. Most species had rows of armour plating along their backs and were strict herbivores.

Scutellosaurus

The name Scutellosaurus, meaning "little-shielded lizard" was a lightly built armoured ornithischian dinosaur found in the early Jurassic period. They weighed only around 10 kilograms, measuring up to 50 centimetres (20 in) in height. The Scuttelosaurs were capable of walking on their hind legs and had an unusually long tail. They were only 4 feet long and were an easy prey for other predators.

Scelidosaurus

The Scelidosauruses lived during the Early Jurassic period and were one of the first armoured dinosaurs to have evolved. Due to shared characteristics with later species, some palaeontologists consider it an early relative of ankylosaurs and nodosaurs. They were plant-eaters with a beak-like snout and rows of osteoderms along its back.

Scelidosaurus

Cretaceous
Armoured Dinosaurs

The armoured dinosaurs of the Cretaceous period were extremely heavily armoured to help escape dangerous predators who walked the Cretaceous lands. They belonged to a family of "armoured beasts" and were completely covered in scaly skin.

Minmi

The Minmi was a small ankylosaur, distinguished by its extensive bony armour. This early Cretaceous herbivore measured around two metres in length and stood approximately one metre tall. Unlike some ankylosaurs, it had relatively long hind limbs compared to its forelimbs, but it was still a slow-moving dinosaur.

Pinacosaurus

The name Pinacosaurus, meaning "plank lizard," refers to a medium-sized ankylosaur from the Late Cretaceous period. These dinosaurs were highly social, often living in large groups. They inhabited arid regions and, as a result, some fossils suggest they may have been buried alive during sandstorms. A collar of armoured plates encircled their neck, while additional plates covered their body and tail.

Pinacosaurus

13

Panoplosaurus

The Panoplosauruses were herbivorous dinosaurs that lived during the Late Cretaceous period and measured between 18 and 25 feet in length. They weighed around four tonnes and stood approximately two metres tall. Unlike some of their relatives, they lacked tail clubs but were covered in heavy armour, with studded plates protecting their backs and tails. It is believed that the Panoplosauruses defended themselves much like modern-day rhinos, using their sheer size and strength to deter predators.

Saichania

The Saichania, meaning "beautiful one," lived about 80 million years ago during the Late Cretaceous period. They were believed to have grazed on tough vegetation due to their exceptionally strong palates. Their tails featured a robust bony structure, which they used to swing at predators. They had short, upward-pointing spikes and always moved in herds. They were shown in the movie Jurassic Park III.

Sauropelta

The Sauropeltas were nodosaur dinosaurs that lived during the Early Cretaceous period. These herbivores appeared surprisingly formidable, despite being plant-eaters. Their upward-pointing spikes made them seem larger than they actually were. Unlike carnivorous dinosaurs, they resembled horned dinosaurs like Triceratops and lacked front teeth. The bony studs covering their bodies were embedded in their skin rather than their skeletons and served as a formidable defence against predators.

Sauropelta

Gastonia

As herbivores, the Gastonias were low-grazing, armoured dinosaurs and among the best-preserved members of their group. They had impressive spikes along their backs, making it difficult for predators to attack from above. Their spiked tails were effective weapons, used to lash at predators during aggressive encounters.

Polacanthus

The Polacanthus are among the earliest-known armoured dinosaurs. They had long, sharp spines along their necks near their heads and shorter spikes protruding from their backs and tails. Weighing around three tonnes, they lived during the Early Cretaceous period. As strict herbivores, they belonged to the ankylosaurian family. Their name, meaning "Many Spikes," reflects their heavily armoured bodies. Measuring 15 feet in length, the Polacanthus lacked tail clubs but had large, fused shields covering their hips.

Hylaeosaurus

The Hylaeosaurus were described as one of the "terrible lizards" and were among the three original dinosaurs identified. Unlike many other armoured dinosaurs, they were likely solitary and did not move in herds. They foraged through bushes and low-lying vegetation in search of plant life to eat. The name Hylaeosaurus, meaning "forest lizard," reflects their heavily spined backs.

Polacanthus

Best Preserved
Fossils

The best-preserved armoured dinosaurs were placed in the Royal Tyrrell Museum in Alberta. The world's best-preserved armoured dinosaurs included an 18-foot-long Nodosaur found in the Alberta sands, which required 7,000 hours of reconstruction work.

Royal Museum

The Nodosaur fossils, after 7,000 hours of reconstruction, are preserved at the Royal Tyrrell Museum in Canada. The fossils were found with their armour and skin still attached. Scientists believe that the Nodosaurs may have been swept away by floods, eventually settling on the ocean floor.

Nodosaur Fossils

110 million years after the Nodosaurs died, their fossils remain among the best-preserved dinosaur specimens ever found. Typically, palaeontologists only recover scattered bones, a skull, or partial remains, leaving the rest of the reconstruction to interpretation. However, this discovery astonished scientists, as the fossils were found intact, including their armour and protective plating. These Nodosaurs weighed around 3,000 pounds and are considered some of the most remarkable fossils ever discovered.

Nodosaur

Camouflaged
Dinosaurs

Most dinosaurs use camouflage to save themselves from predators. Today, animals such as chameleons, octopuses, and stick insects use camouflage. These dinosaurs experience high predation pressure from large beasts like the Tyrannosaurus Rex. Camouflage in dinosaurs was also used for social signalling.

Psittacosaurus

The Psittacosaurs were first discovered in Mongolia and are said to have lived around 110 million years ago. The name Psittacosaurus, meaning "Parrot Lizard," comes from their parrot-like appearance. They used their powerful, parrot-like beaks to crack seeds and nuts. Their bodies exhibited counter-shading camouflage, which helped reduce shadows and provided a defensive advantage.

Borealopelta

These heavily armoured dinosaurs had a reddish-brown camouflage to trick predators into overlooking them in their environment. They lived about 110 million years ago and had a distinctive red and white counter-shading pattern. Although these armoured dinosaurs were at risk of being hunted by larger predators like T. rex, their camouflage abilities helped them avoid detection to some extent.

Psittacosaurus

Bulletproof
Armour

It is said that the armour of dinosaurs and modern-day animals like crocodiles and turtles, which have bone-like plates, was actually derived from hardened skin structures called osteoderms. Ankylosaurs were the most well-known dinosaurs with osteoderms covering their skin, while their primitive ancestors had much thinner armour.

Stegosaurus

The Stegosaurs were among the most famous armoured dinosaurs of the Late Jurassic period. Their name, meaning "roofed lizard," refers to the two rows of large bony plates along their backs, which were believed to be osteoderm projections. These large, plant-eating dinosaurs had relatively small brains, with some estimates suggesting that the brain of a Stegosaur was the size of a walnut. The largest Stegosaurian species grew up to 30 feet in length.

Aetosaur

The Aetosaurs, meaning "eagle lizard", were a group of heavily armoured herbivores that lived during the Late Triassic period. They had small heads, upturned snouts, and bodies covered with plate-like scutes. These scutes were osteoderm projections embedded in their skin. Their skulls resembled those of modern birds. Growing up to five metres in length, they had long, narrow bodies resembling crocodiles and are believed to be closely related to modern crocodilians.

Stegosaurus

Thyreophorans

The Thyreophorans were a group of ornithischian or bird-hipped dinosaurs that included all types of armoured dinosaurs. They walked on all fours and were complete plant-eaters. This group included Ankylosaurs and Stegosaurs as well. Some of the Thyreophorans, meaning "Shield Bearers" are Kentrosaurus, Tatisaurus and Emausaurus.

Emausaurus

The Emausauruses originated in the Early Jurassic period, and the only known fossil belonged to a juvenile. This specimen was about two metres long and is believed to have been an intermediate form between Scutellosaurus and Scelidosaurus. They would have grazed on low-lying vegetation, and adult Emausauruses were estimated to grow up to four metres in length.

Kentrosaurus

The Kentrosauruses were Stegosaurian dinosaurs that lived during the Late Jurassic period. They were capable of swinging their tails at speeds of up to 80 kilometres per hour to defend themselves against predators. They possessed formidable weaponry, with a double row of plates and spikes along their backs. Their hind legs were twice as long as their front legs, allowing them to rear up on their hind limbs to reach high vegetation.

Kentrosaurus

Stegosaurian
Dinosaurs

The Stegosauruses were a group of armoured dinosaurs that had similar bony spikes and spines lined along their backs. They lived around 150 million years ago during the Late Jurassic period. These dinosaurs were large, heavily built herbivores with short necks and massive bodies. The most recognisable feature of the Stegosauruses was their distinctive plates and flat spines along their backs.

Chialingosaurus

The Chialingosauruses were herbivorous Stegosaurian dinosaurs that shared similarities with Kentrosauruses. The name "Chialing lizard" refers to one of the oldest species in the Stegosaurian group. They had spikes arranged from their backs to their tails, which helped them identify others of their species. These spikes also served as a defence mechanism against hungry raptors.

Regnosaurus

The Regnosauruses, meaning "Sussex Lizards," were herbivorous Stegosaurian dinosaurs that lived during the Early Cretaceous period. They were estimated to be around four metres long, but limited fossil evidence has resulted in many unknown details about this dinosaur. Some scientists speculate that the Regnosauruses may have been closely related to Sauropods.

Regnosaurus

Jiangjunosaurus

The Jiangjunosauruses were herbivorous Stegosaurians that lived during the Late Jurassic period. They reached around six metres in length and weighed approximately 2.5 tonnes. Predatory threats to the Jiangjunosauruses included Sinraptors and other theropods that coexisted in the same ecosystem.

Huayangosaurus

The Huayangosauruses were smaller, plated dinosaurs with a series of plates running down their backs, gradually transforming into spikes near their tails. Their tails ended with four massive spikes, which they used to defend themselves against predators. The Huayangosauruses had long, slender heads and short front legs, allowing them to graze on low-lying vegetation.

Paranthodon

The Paranthodons lived in South Africa during the Early Cretaceous period, around 145 million years ago. They were among the first known dinosaurs to have inhabited Africa. These Stegosaurian dinosaurs weighed approximately two tonnes and grew up to 16 feet in length. They were low-browsing dinosaurs closely related to the Stegosauruses. Like other Stegosaurians, they had spikes running along their backs.

Jiangjunosaurus

Mesozoic Armoured
Armour

The Ankylosaurs and the Nodosauruses were the most common and famous armoured dinosaurs of the Mesozoic era. Around 40 different species of armoured dinosaurs thrived during prehistoric times. They were the well-defended herbivores of the Mesozoic.

Acanthopholis

The Acanthopholises, meaning "spiny scales," lived during the mid-Cretaceous period. They grew up to 13 feet long and weighed around 800 pounds. These dinosaurs had oval-shaped armour and beaked mouths. They belonged to the Ankylosaur family and were typical examples of Nodosauruses. Their dangerous-looking spikes on their necks, shoulders, and tails served as a strong defence against large Cretaceous carnivores.

Dracopelta

The Dracopeltas, meaning "Dragon Shield" dinosaurs, lived during the Late Jurassic period. These herbivores measured about six feet in length and weighed around 200 pounds. Like all Ankylosaurs, the Dracopeltas were relatively slow and clumsy dinosaurs. When sensing danger, they would flop onto their stomachs and curl into a tightly armoured ball to deter predators.

Acanthopholis

Clubbed Tail
Dinosaurs

The Ankylosaurs were among the most well-known clubbed-tail armoured dinosaurs. The primary function of their clubbed tails were to fend off large predators, including Tyrannosaurus rex and other Theropods. These tails had a bony structure that allowed Ankylosaurs to swing them forcefully, often striking and crippling the hind limbs of attacking predators. Many other species of armoured dinosaurs also evolved with this defensive feature.

Talarurus

The Talaruruses lived in Mongolia during the Late Cretaceous period. They were armoured herbivores that grew up to 20 feet in length. These dinosaurs had broad skulls and bony armour embedded in their skin, known as osteoderms, which helped them evade large predators. They were particularly known for using their clubbed tails to defend themselves.

Ziapelta

The Ziapeltas were an extinct group of Ankylosaurid dinosaurs that lived during the Late Cretaceous period. They were discovered in New Mexico and identified as plant-eaters. Unlike many other Ankylosaurs, they were not just armoured but heavily fortified, featuring shoulder spikes and large bony clubs at the ends of their tails._ Their most distinct feature was the series of large, pointed spikes that lined their backs.

Ziapelta

Armoured
Insectivores

Although most armoured dinosaurs were herbivores, some evidence suggests that a few species may have fed on small insects. While almost all Ankylosaurs, Nodosauruses, and other armoured dinosaurs relied on low-lying vegetation, there are a handful of species believed to have included insects in their diet. However, there is no known evidence of armoured dinosaurs being carnivorous in nature.

Albertosaurus

The Albertosauruses were Theropod dinosaurs that lived during the Late Cretaceous period. Some scientists speculate that these dinosaurs may have had armoured tails, which they used to whip away predators. They were classified as insectivores and, like all other Theropods, walked exclusively on their two hind legs. Although they are not traditionally classified as armoured dinosaurs, some researchers suggest they may fit into the category due to the presence of light protective structures on their bodies.

Lametasaurus

The Lametasauruses, also known as Lambiosauruses, were believed to be armoured insectivores. These duck-billed dinosaurs possessed light armour covering parts of their bodies. They had thick, leathery skin that provided some protection against predators attempting to pierce through it.

Lametasaurus

CERATOP DINOSAURS

Ceratop Dinosaurs

The Ceratopses, meaning "horned faces," were herbivorous dinosaurs that lived during the Late Cretaceous period. They were beaked dinosaurs with spectacular horns that inhabited North America. Easily recognisable by the structure of their skulls, they also had parrot-like beaks and large nasal horns. Early Ceratopsians were small bipedal dinosaurs from the Late Jurassic, but they evolved into large horned species only in the Late Cretaceous.

Psittacosaurus

The Psittacosauruses were notable for being the most species-rich group of Ceratopsian dinosaurs in history. Their name, meaning "parrot lizard," was given due to their parrot-like beaks. They walked on their hind limbs and used their forelimbs for grasping objects. Assumed to be fast runners, they may have reached speeds comparable to an ostrich. They weighed between 30 and 100 kilograms and had small horns on their cheeks. Their unique head structure suggests that they may have cared for their young before leaving their nests.

Chaoyangsaurus

The Chaoyangsauruses date back to the Late Jurassic period and were identified as Ceratopsians due to their horny beaks. Alongside Psittacosauruses, they were among the earliest-known Ceratopsians. They remained small, growing up to three feet in length.

Psittacosaurus

Triceratops

The Triceratopses were herbivorous dinosaurs that first appeared during the Late Cretaceous period. They were known as the largest of the horned dinosaurs. Their name, meaning "three-horned face," reflects their enormous horns and large frills. Although they were heavily armoured, they were occasionally preyed upon by Tyrannosaurus rex.

Torosaurus

It is commonly believed that Torosauruses were actually fully grown Triceratopses. Unlike Triceratopses, their frills contained large holes, which are thought to have enlarged as they matured. They lived during the Cretaceous period and grew up to nine metres long. The name Torosaurus, meaning "bull lizard," refers to their massive skulls and large bony frills at the backs of their heads. They weighed around eight tonnes.

Diet

The Triceratopses were plant-eating dinosaurs that grazed on low-lying vegetation. Their nasal horns were used for defence. Weighing around five tonnes, they fed primarily on shrubs and other low-growing plants. Their beak-like mouths were well-suited for grasping and plucking vegetation rather than biting and tearing. It is likely that they also used their large horns to tip over trees for food.

Torosaurus

Protoceratops

The Protoceratopses were a group of sheep-sized dinosaurs from the Upper Cretaceous period. They were well-known for being a frequent prey of Velociraptors. Unlike most Ceratopsians, they lacked large horns but had small bony bumps on their snouts. They had strong jaws that enabled them to bite through tough vegetation. Weighing around 200 kilograms, they were significantly smaller than their larger relatives. The first dinosaur eggs ever discovered belonged to Protoceratopses.

Chasmosaurus

The Chasmosauruses were mid-sized Ceratopsian dinosaurs that primarily fed on plants. Their name, meaning "open lizard," comes from the large openings in their frills. They were capable of running at speeds comparable to modern-day rhinos. Living during the Cretaceous period, they possessed three facial horns and had thick, barrel-shaped bodies. Measuring up to 26 feet in length, they fed on seed ferns, cycads, and shrubs. They relied on their heads and horns to protect themselves from predators.

Chasmosaurus

Basal Ceratops

The basal ceratops were known to have no horns and date back to the Late Jurassic period, living in North America. The most distinctive features of basal ceratops were their frilled skulls. Although they did have long nasal horns, they were the most primitive types of dinosaurs.

Yinlong

The Yinlongs were basal Ceratopsians, meaning "hidden dragon." They lived during the Late Jurassic period and were small, bipedal herbivorous dinosaurs. Measuring just one metre in length and weighing about 15 kilograms, they were among the smallest Ceratopsians. They were also known for storing stones in their stomachs to aid digestion and plant-grinding.

Hualianceratops

The Hualianceratopses were herbivorous Ceratopsians that lived around 160 million years ago. Their name, meaning "ornamental face," refers to the decorative structures on their skulls. These hornless, basal Ceratopsians lived in China and were distant relatives of Triceratopses. About the size of a spaniel, they walked on their hind legs. They were among the earliest Ceratopsians of the Late Jurassic period.

Yinlong

Neoceratopsia

The Neoceratopses were large herbivorous dinosaurs that primarily moved in herds. They adapted to a wide range of habitats, including forests, swamps, savannas, and semi-polar regions. Their most common defensive tactic against predators was shaking their frills and displaying their horns. If a predator did not retreat, they would charge ferociously. They had selective appetites, feeding on plant matter ranging from tall grasses to woody stems.

Liaoceratops

The Liaoceratopses were the most primitive, hare-sized, and oldest Neoceratopsians ever discovered. They were distant cousins of Triceratopses and stood about one foot tall, measuring less than three feet in length. They had small, sideways-facing horns beneath their eyes and a short, thick frill on their skulls. Due to their small size and lack of defensive features, Liaoceratopses were easily preyed upon by larger predators.

Liaoceratops

Top Ceratopsian
Dinosaurs

The ceratopsian dinosaurs like the Triceratops, Protoceratops and Pentaceratops were most commonly known as the top ceratopsian dinosaurs. Although these ceratops dominated the Jurassic and Cretaceous periods, there were a few Ceratopsian dinosaurs that were prominently present.

Styracosaurus

The Styracosauruses were one of the best-known Ceratopsian dinosaurs, classified as Centrosaurines. These herbivorous dinosaurs lived during the Cretaceous period. Their name, meaning "spiked lizard," refers to their impressive head structures, which featured prominent horns and frills. They had a two-foot-long nasal horn and weighed up to three tonnes, resembling modern elephants in size. They travelled in herds, using their frills as signals to communicate with one another.

Achelousaurus

The Achelousauruses were Ceratopsian dinosaurs that lived during the Late Cretaceous period. They measured up to 20 feet in length and weighed around one tonne. These medium-sized dinosaurs had bony knobs above their eyes and large frills. Despite their intimidating appearance, they were gentle plant-eaters.

Styracosaurus

Zuniceratops

The Zuniceratopses, meaning "Zuni-horned face," were Ceratopsian dinosaurs that lived during the Late Cretaceous period. They were small, horned herbivores that weighed around 150 kilograms and grew up to three metres in length. They were the earliest known Ceratopsians to develop eyebrow horns and were also believed to have nasal horns. They lived in herds and were closely related to Triceratopses.

Pachyrhinosaurus

The Pachyrhinosauruses, meaning "thick-nosed lizards," were extinct Ceratopsians that lived during the Late Cretaceous period. They measured about eight metres in length and weighed approximately four tonnes. Unlike most Ceratopsians, they lacked prominent horns and instead had thick, flattened skull bones with a large nasal boss. Their facial humps, known as "bosses," were used for headbutting during fights. They had long cheek teeth that helped them grind and chew tough vegetation.

Pachyrhinosaurus

Centrosaurus

The Centrosauruses were large herbivorous Ceratopsians. Their name, meaning "pointed lizard," refers to their single long horn located at the tip of their snout. They measured around 20 feet in length and weighed approximately three tonnes. Unlike Triceratopses, which had three horns, and Pentaceratopses, which had five, Centrosauruses relied on their single horn primarily for signalling rather than defence. Herds of Centrosauruses are believed to have perished in flash floods.

Einiosaurus

The Einiosauruses were medium-sized Ceratopsians that lived during the Upper Cretaceous period. They weighed about 1.3 tonnes and grew up to six metres in length. A pair of large spikes projected backwards from their small frills. They were the earliest known Ceratopsians to develop nasal horns, which evolved into "bosses" in later Ceratopsians. They had an unusually curved nasal horn, which may have been a transitional feature in the evolution of later Ceratopsian species.

Einiosaurus

The Ceratopsian dinosaurs first evolved during the Late Jurassic period and thrived until the Late Cretaceous period. Dinosaurs such as Triceratops, Chasmosaurus, and Psittacosaurus emerged during the Late Jurassic. These early Ceratopsians played a crucial role in the evolution of later species with elaborate horns and frills.

Xuanhuaceratops

The Xuanhuaceratopses were an early genus of Ceratopsian dinosaurs that evolved during the Late Jurassic period. They were among the earliest-known Ceratopsians and were discovered in China. They shared many features with Chaoyangsauruses and were small, bipedal herbivores. They developed sharp cropping beaks and had basic frills, which later evolved into dominant features in more advanced Ceratopsians.

Albertaceratops

The Albertaceratopses were horned Ceratopsian dinosaurs with unusually long brow horns. Unlike most Ceratopsians, which typically had short brow horns, Albertaceratopses featured elongated ones. They were basal Ceratopsians, distinguished by two small horns positioned at the top of their frills. The Albertaceratopses have since been reclassified under the genus Medusaceratops.

Albertaceratops

Auroraceratop

The Auroraceratopses, meaning "dawn-horned face," were basal Neoceratopsians from the Early Cretaceous period. Most Neoceratopsians had long, narrow snouts, but Auroraceratopses were distinct due to their shorter, wider skulls. Their most unique trait was the presence of two pairs of teeth, which may have been used for digging and gripping plants.

Leptoceratops

The Leptoceratopses were early, primitive Ceratopsians that exhibited some unique traits. Fossil evidence suggests that some specimens were preserved in a "clapping hands" position, leading scientists to hypothesize that they may have walked on their hind legs while using their forelimbs for grasping food and plants. They were herbivores believed to have lived in mountainous and hilly regions. Their tails were leaf-shaped, adding to their distinct appearance.

Montanoceratops

The Montanoceratopses were small Ceratopsian dinosaurs discovered in Alberta. They roamed across a vast territory and had hind legs that were larger than their forelimbs, giving them an arched back when walking on all fours. They had short tails, common head frills, and a single horn.

Montanoceratops

Prenoceratops

The Prenoceratopses lived during the Late Cretaceous period and grew up to three metres long. They inhabited North America and were closely related to Leptoceratopses. They can be distinguished by their skulls, which had a distinct forward slope. As ground-dwelling herbivores, they primarily fed on low-lying vegetation. Their name, meaning "bent forward" or "prone-horned face," refers to their unique skull shape. They lived approximately 83 million years ago.

Platyceratop

The Platyceratopses were herbivorous Ceratopsians that lived during the Late Cretaceous period. Their name, meaning "flat-horned face," refers to the unique shape of their skulls. They measured roughly one metre in length and exhibited basal traits. Closely resembling Bagaceratopses, they also had parrot-like beaks.

Turanoceratops

The Turanoceratopses were relatively small dinosaurs, weighing around 175 kilograms. They lived during the Late Cretaceous period and were herbivorous Ceratopsians. Their skulls bore long brow horns, a feature distinguishing them from other early Ceratopsians. They grew up to two metres long and displayed several basal traits. With parrot-like beaks, they were true members of the Ceratopsian family, primarily feeding on ferns and conifers.

Prenoceratops

Montana
Ceratops

Ceratopsian fossils have been discovered scattered across Montana, with numerous specimens excavated from Montana's fossil-rich sands. Many Triceratopses, Theropods, and other dinosaurs have been unearthed in this region.

Baby Ava

A small baby dinosaur resembling a miniature Triceratops was recently discovered in Montana. This complete Triceratops-relative, informally named "Ava," was estimated to have lived 75 million years ago during the Cretaceous period. Unlike adult Triceratopses, it lacked a nasal horn. Due to its similarities to Avaceratopses, scientists decided to name this species "Ava."

Judith Dinosaur

A new Ceratopsian fossil discovered in the Judith River rock formation in Montana has led to the classification of a new species, officially named Spiclypeus shipporum. Nicknamed "Judith," this dinosaur lived approximately 76 million years ago. It was believed to be 15 feet long, weighing up to four tonnes. A close relative of Triceratopses, it had prominent facial horns and head frills.

Judith

Ancient Beasts

Ceratopsians were famous for their horns and frills and appeared frightening when charging at predators. Despite being herbivores, they successfully defended themselves from large predators. With their heavy bodies and horned faces, they closely resembled modern-day rhinos and elephants. Over time, scientists have discovered more Ceratopsians with even fiercer horns, some of which were among the most intimidating dinosaurs to have ever lived.

Kosmoceratops

The Kosmoceratopses had nearly 15 full-sized horns on their heads and lived during the Cretaceous period, approximately 76 million years ago. They had enormous skulls, measuring two metres in length, and weighed around 2.5 tonnes. Resembling oversized rhinos, they had large, pointed horns used for defence against predators. Among all known dinosaurs, they were considered one of the most ornamented Ceratopsians.

Titanoceratops

The Titanoceratopses were giant Ceratopsians, weighing approximately seven tonnes. They lived around 76 million years ago and are considered one of the earliest known relatives of Triceratopses. They had thinner frills, longer noses, and larger horns compared to Triceratopses.

Kosmoceratop

Spectacular Horned
Dinosaurs

Ceratopsians were famous for their elaborate horns and frills. Among them, Triceratopses were the most common and widely recognised horned dinosaurs. Many Ceratopsians displayed bizarre and fascinating skull ornamentation, making them some of the most visually striking dinosaurs in history.

Eotriceratops

The Eotriceratopses, meaning "early Triceratops," had spiky frills and two long brow horns. They were among the largest Ceratopsians, with skulls that were claimed to weigh as much as a car. Growing up to 10 metres in length and exceeding the weight of a Tyrannosaurus rex, they were the largest horned dinosaurs. They also had a short nasal horn.

Medusaceratops

The Medusaceratopses were distinguished by strangely curved horns on their frills. Measuring about seven metres in length, they were originally mistaken for Albertaceratopses. Their name, meaning "Medusa-horned face," refers to the resemblance of their hooked horns to the mythical snake-haired Medusa. They lived approximately 77 million years ago and were discovered in Montana.

Eotriceratops

Diabloceratops

The Diabloceratopses, meaning "devil-horned faces," were primitive Ceratopsians found in Utah. They had small nasal horns but large brow horns, along with even larger curved horns extending from their frills. Their unique forward-curving frill gave them an unusual appearance. Possessing massive jaws and powerful beaks, they were formidable defenders against predators.

Rubeosaurus

The Rubeosauruses had large nasal horns that they used as defensive weapons. Unlike modern rhinos, whose horns are made of keratin, Rubeosauruses had horns composed of solid bone. They also had straight horns protruding from their frills, giving them an intimidating appearance. They were initially thought to be a species of Styracosaurus.

Coahuilaceratops

The Coahuilaceratopses were closely related to Pentaceratopses and possessed a small nasal horn with massive brow horns. Weighing around five tonnes and measuring seven metres long, they resembled modern elephants. Their brow horns were the largest of any known Ceratopsian species.

Kosmoceratop

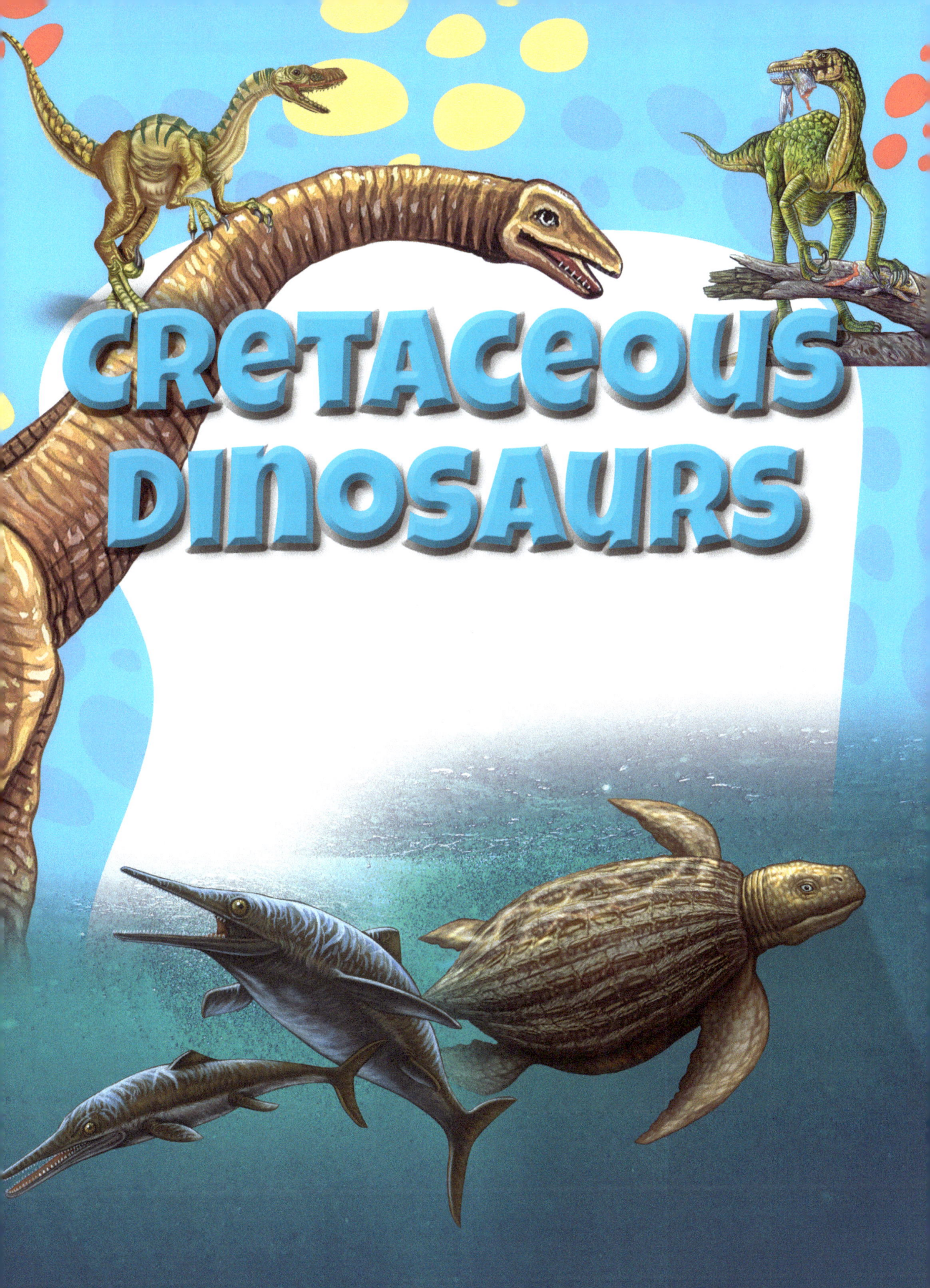

CRETACEOUS DINOSAURS

The Cretaceous
Period

The period between 145.5 and 65.5 million years ago is known as the Cretaceous Period. It marked the final period of the Mesozoic Era. At the beginning of the Cretaceous Period, the supercontinent Pangaea began to break apart into smaller land masses. By the mid-Cretaceous period, Pangaea had fragmented into multiple continents, leading to the diversification of land-based life. This continental drift triggered climatic changes, making the Cretaceous period cooler than previous eras.

Mass Extinction

The forests of the Cretaceous period closely resembled modern forests. Toward the end of this period, a massive asteroid impact led to the extinction of nearly half of the world's species. While some scientists believe this extinction was caused by long-term environmental changes, the asteroid impact remains the most widely accepted theory. This extinction event, occurring around 65 million years ago, marked the end of the Mesozoic Era and led to the extinction of non-avian dinosaurs, leaving only birds as their surviving relatives.

Ceratopsian
Dinosaurs

The Ceratopsians, or "bird-hipped" dinosaurs, emerged during the Cretaceous period approximately 140 million years ago. They evolved into species with massive horns and frills. Ceratopsians flourished in the Late Cretaceous period, adapting to various environments. Their cheek teeth suggest they had a rough plant-based diet, consuming tough vegetation. Among them, the Triceratops became one of the most well-known species.

Centrosaurus

The Centrosauruses lived around 75 million years ago and were large, horned herbivorous dinosaurs. They traveled in large herds in search of food and water. Centrosauruses had beak-like mouths, large horns near their snouts, and thick skulls above their eyes. Their skin was covered in scales, similar to modern reptiles.

Chasmosaurus

The Chasmosauruses, meaning "opening lizards," were medium-sized Ceratopsians weighing around two tonnes. Their most distinctive feature was their large, frill-shaped skull, adorned with three facial horns—one on the nose and two above the eyes. Their skin displayed large scales, adding to their intimidating appearance. The Chasmosauruses were among the first Ceratopsians ever discovered.

Chasmosaurus

Protoceratops

The Protoceratopses were sheep-sized Ceratopsians and belonged to an early group of horned dinosaurs. Their name, meaning "First Horned Face," reflects their early place in Ceratopsian evolution. Much smaller than later Ceratopsians, they were frequent prey for Velociraptors. Fossil evidence suggests that Protoceratopses may have been buried by sandstorms, leading to the mass preservation of their remains.

Torosaurus

The Torosauruses lived around 70 million years ago during the Late Cretaceous period. These plant-eating dinosaurs had large, bony frills with distinctive holes. They measured approximately 25 feet in length and stood eight feet tall. The Torosauruses, meaning "bull lizards," weighed around eight tonnes and had toothless beaks and massive bodies.

Styracosaurus

The Styracosauruses, meaning "spiked lizards," were among the most spectacular horned dinosaurs. They possessed multiple long, dramatic horns on their skulls, including a two-foot-long nasal horn and were considered the most attractive for species of the same kind. Their frills served multiple functions, including thermoregulation, species communication, and chasing away other attacking predators. A fully grown Styracosaurus weighed up to three tonnes and moved in large herds.

Styracosaurus

Avians

By the mid-Cretaceous period, ancient birds evolved, coexisting with Pterosaurs in the skies. Two major theories explain the evolution of flight: the Trees-Down Theory and the Ground-Up Theory. The Trees-Down Theory suggests that small reptiles evolved flight by gliding from trees, while the Ground-Up Theory proposes that small theropods developed flight by leaping to catch prey. Feathers are believed to have initially evolved for thermoregulation, later adapting for flight.

Diversification

Avians were highly successful and diversified during the Cretaceous period. One example is Confuciusornis, a crow-sized bird that lived 125 million years ago. It had modern beak-like features and enormous claws at the tips of its wings, designed for capturing prey. Another species, Iberomesornis, was sparrow-sized and capable of sustained flight. Some evidence suggests that Iberomesornis may have been insectivorous.

Confuciusornis

Herbivorous
Dinosaurs

Massive herds of ornithischian herbivores, such as Iguanodons, Ankylosauruses, and Ceratopsians, thrived during the Cretaceous period. Iguanodons belonged to a group of duck-billed dinosaurs, also known as Hadrosaurs. Dinosaurs such as Apatosauruses and Diplodocuses had already gone extinct by this time. Meanwhile, Theropods like Tyrannosaurus rex (T-Rex) remained the dominant apex predators until the end of the Cretaceous era.

Sauropods

By the end of the Jurassic period, large Sauropods, such as Apatosauruses and Diplodocuses, went extinct. However, some giant Sauropods, including Titanosaurs, thrived toward the end of the Cretaceous period. Sauropods were characterised by their long necks, small heads, and four sturdy legs. They first appeared during the Late Triassic period.

The name Sauropod, meaning "lizard-footed dinosaur,". They were among the largest terrestrial animals to have ever lived, including some dwarf Sauropod species. Most Sauropods grew up to 110 feet in length. The longest-known dinosaur, Argentinosaurus huinculensis, reached an estimated length of 130 feet on average.

Argentinosaurus

Baryonyx

The Baryonyxes lived during the Early Cretaceous period, approximately 130 million years ago. They were among the largest fish-eating dinosaurs to have ever walked the planet. Their name, meaning "Heavy Claw," reflects their enormous, curved claws. Weighing around two tonnes, they primarily hunted in rivers and lakes. With their crocodile-like, they were highly specialised hunters.

Suchomimus

The Suchomimuses were large Spinosaurid dinosaurs that lived 125 million years ago during the Early Cretaceous period. They were notable for their large sail-like structure on their backs, positioned near the tail. Suchomimuses had massive claws on their forelimbs, which they used to catch fish. Their elongated, crocodile-like snouts and foot-long claws on each thumb further aided in their hunting abilities. Their name means "Crocodile Mimic".

Oviraptors

The Oviraptors, meaning "Egg Thieves," were feathered Mongolian Theropods that lived during the Cretaceous period. They were given this name by paleontologists who initially discovered their fossils atop Protoceratops eggs, mistakenly believing they had been stealing them. However, later studies revealed that Oviraptors actually brooded their own eggs, similar to modern birds. They were classified as bird-mimic dinosaurs and lived alongside Velociraptors. They had long legs built for speed, a large, toothless beak, and a body covered in feathers.

Baryonyx

Abelisaurids

The Abelisaurids were unusual Theropods from the Cretaceous period. They had extremely strong necks, disproportionately small arms, and rigid backbones. Their hunting style involved using their powerful jaws to seize prey and shaking it vigorously from side to side. This aggressive method allowed them to rip apart flesh and even dismember their prey.

Majungasaurus

The Majungasauruses were medium-sized Abelisaurids that lived in Madagascar at the end of the Cretaceous period. They were known for their lumpy skulls and carnivorous diet. They had unusually short legs, broad shoulder blades, and tiny forearms. Fossil evidence suggests that their spinal columns contained air sacs, indicating a bird-like respiratory system.

Rugops

Although only partial fossils of the Rugops have been discovered, scientists have been able to estimate their weight and skeletal structure. These scavengers measured around 18 feet in length and weighed approximately two tonnes. They primarily fed on carcasses left behind by larger predators. Despite their resemblance to Tyrannosauruses, they lived around 95 million years ago during the Late Cretaceous period.

Majungasaurus

Rajasaurus

The Rajasauruses were Abelisaurian dinosaurs that lived 70 million years ago during the Late Cretaceous period. Their name, meaning "King of Lizards," reflects their formidable predatory nature. These large carnivores measured approximately 30 feet long and 10 feet tall. With a large skull and a unique head crest, they stood apart from other dinosaurs. Rajasauruses primarily hunted Sauropods but were also known to scavenge on dead dinosaurs.

Skorpiovenator

Skorpiovenator, meaning "Scorpion Hunter," was a large carnivorous theropod from the Late Cretaceous period. Though not as famous as Tyrannosaurus rex or Allosaurus, it was equally terrifying and just as deadly. This powerful dinosaur coexisted with other fearsome predators and earned its name because its fossils were found surrounded by scorpions, adding an eerie and mysterious element to its discovery.

Rajasaurus

Large Mammals
Dominance

The Tyrannosaurus Rex, commonly known as T-Rex, was the king of dinosaurs and one of the most beloved prehistoric creatures. It emerged around 80 million years ago during the Cretaceous period and remained the top land predator until dinosaurs went extinct 20 million years later. While the mighty T-Rex ruled the north, the Spinosaurus, a monstrous meat-eater with a sail-like fin on its back measuring up to two metres, dominated the south. This fin likely displayed dominance and attracted mates. Meanwhile, the skies were ruled by large Pterosaurs, making the prehistoric world a dangerous and fascinating place.

The Giants

The warm, shallow seas paved the way for new landmasses to split apart and emerge. The long-necked plesiosaurs preceded the giant, snake-like mosasaurs. Towards the end of the Cretaceous period, horned beasts such as the Triceratops emerged, which primarily fed on cycads and other low-lying plants. During this time, diatoms, a type of shelled plankton, underwent their first major radiation into the ocean.

Spinosaurus

Elasmosaurus

One of the most remarkable-looking sea creatures that appeared during the Cretaceous period was the Elasmosaurus. This marine reptile had a unique advantage—its prey could not see the huge body hidden on the other side of its long neck. The Elasmosaurus fed on smaller fish. Like all plesiosaurs, the Elasmosaurus ingested small stones to help grind its food. Elasmosaurs travelled long distances collecting stones to aid in digestion and to stabilise their body weight.

Sea Monsters

Categorised as a 'sea monster', the Megalodon was one of the most ferocious sharks, although it actually lived during the Cenozoic Era, not the Cretaceous. Another shark, called the Squalicorax, had eyesight similar to that of humans and was also referred to as the 'Crow Shark'. The giant squid of the Cretaceous period measured between 23 and 30 metres in length and thrived in warm waters. The Xiphactinus, often called the 'Bulldog Fish', grew up to six metres (20 feet) long. It was an exceptionally fast swimmer, reaching speeds of up to 64 km/h (40 mph).

Megalodon

Aquatic Reptiles

The Ichthyosaurs, Mosasaurs, Plesiosaurs, and most invertebrate marine animals were wiped out by the mass extinction event at the end of the Cretaceous period. Although this extinction was smaller in scale compared to the mass extinction during the Permian-Triassic period, it was significant enough to mark the end of the Age of Reptiles and the beginning of the Age of Mammals.

Mosasaurs

The Mosasaurs were an extinct group of carnivorous aquatic lizards that lived during the Cretaceous period and dominated the Cretaceous seas. Despite their size and fearsome teeth, they were not dinosaurs. Their formidable array of teeth allowed them to tear into fish, birds, and other aquatic reptiles.

Ichthyosaurus

The Ichthyosaurus, meaning "fish lizard", was a large marine reptile that thrived primarily during the Jurassic period, not the Cretaceous. While dinosaurs dominated the land, the Ichthyosaurs ruled the seas. They were not dinosaurs but a distinct group of marine reptiles. They were among the fastest swimming marine creatures, perfectly adapted for speed.

Ichthyosaurus

Plesiosaurs

The Plesiosaurs were a diverse group of extinct marine reptiles that lived during the Mesozoic Era, including the Cretaceous period. The name 'Plesiosaur' means 'near lizard'. They were carnivorous, primarily feeding on smaller fish and molluscs. It is believed that some Plesiosaurs gave birth to live young rather than laying eggs. They measured around 4.5 metres (15 feet) in length and weighed approximately two tonnes. Their most distinguishing features were their elongated necks and streamlined bodies.

Xiphactinus

The Xiphactinus was a formidable predator, known for its speed and aggressive hunting style. It was capable of leaping out of the water, similar to modern dolphins. Often referred to as the 'killer fish', it had massive, interlocking teeth. Growing up to six metres (20 feet) in length and weighing around a third of a tonne, the Xiphactinus was one of the fastest marine predators of its time, reaching speeds of up to 64 km/h (40 mph).

Archelon

The Archelon, a prehistoric sea turtle, weighed over two tonnes and had a shell span of up to 5.5 metres (18 feet). The largest turtle to have ever existed, it primarily fed on jellyfish and ammonites, occasionally grazing on seaweed. These turtles returned to land only to mate and lay eggs. They lived around 75 million years ago and spent much of their time resting on the seabed. Possessing a powerful, hooked beak, they were capable of biting through flesh and bone with immense force.

Archelon

Triceratops

The Triceratops, meaning "three-horned face", is one of the most recognisable dinosaurs of the Cretaceous period. It grew up to nine metres in length and weighed up to 10 tonnes. The Triceratops was a herbivore, using its strong beak to shear through tough vegetation.

Velociraptor

The Velociraptor, meaning "quick plunderer", was a lightweight and highly agile predator. It weighed up to 15 kg and measured up to 1.8 metres in length. It is now widely accepted that these dinosaurs were covered in feathers. During the Jurassic period, similar `raptor' species grew larger in size, resembling Deinonychus.

T.Rex

The most well-known giant dinosaur, the Tyrannosaurus Rex, or "Tyrant Lizard King", was a fearsome apex predator. It grew up to 12 metres in length and weighed approximately five tonnes. T. rex lived during the Late Cretaceous period. These dinosaurs could open their jaws up to one metre wide. Their teeth were serrated and capable of crushing bone as well as tearing flesh. T. rex had keen hearing, an acute sense of smell, and sharp eyesight, making it an efficient hunter.

Velociraptor

Fish Hunters

Toothed Bird

The Hesperornis, or the "Toothed Bird", was a common species during the Late Cretaceous period. This species was flightless and had limited mobility on land, spending most of its time hunting fish and squid. Hesperornis laid eggs and was a skilled marine predator. It measured up to 1.8 metres (six feet) in length. Unlike modern birds, its brain was relatively small.

Ankylosaur

The Ankylosaurs had a distinctive, heavily armoured body with osteoderms (bony plates) covering their back. They were originally believed to be strict herbivores, but recent fossil evidence has suggested that some species may have consumed fish as well. They lived during the Early Cretaceous period, approximately 125 million years ago.

Liaoningosaurus

The Liaoningosaurus, sometimes referred to as the "Liaoning lizard", exhibited a mix of features from both nodosaurs and ankylosaurs. Initially believed to be herbivorous, fossil evidence later revealed that it was a fish-eater. This small dinosaur, measuring only 34 centimetres in length, was one of the smallest known armoured dinosaurs. It lived during the Early Cretaceous period and has been nicknamed the `Aptian dinosaur' due to its age.

Hesperornis

New Dinosaurs

Animal life developed similar to that of the Jurassic period. During the Cretaceous period, new species of dinosaurs evolved. Example: Ceratopsians, a group of plant-eating Ornithischian dinosaurs. These dinosaurs had bird-like hip structures. The most famous example of this group is Triceratops, which possessed three horns and a large bony frill that extended from its skull.

Ornithischian

The Ornithischians were a diverse group of herbivorous dinosaurs that fed exclusively on plants and could grow up to 10 metres in length. They had an extra jaw bone, the predentary. The name 'Ornithischian' means 'bird-hipped', though these dinosaurs were not closely related to modern birds. One of the most well-known Ornithischians was the Stegosaurus; it lived during the Jurassic period.

New Era

Although many species perished during the mass extinction event at the end of the Cretaceous, some life persisted into the next geological age --the Cenozoic Era. This era, often referred to as the `Age of Mammals', saw the rise of new and small mammals. With the extinction of large reptiles, mammals began to dominate terrestrial ecosystems and ultimately became the ruling class of life on Earth.

Triceratop

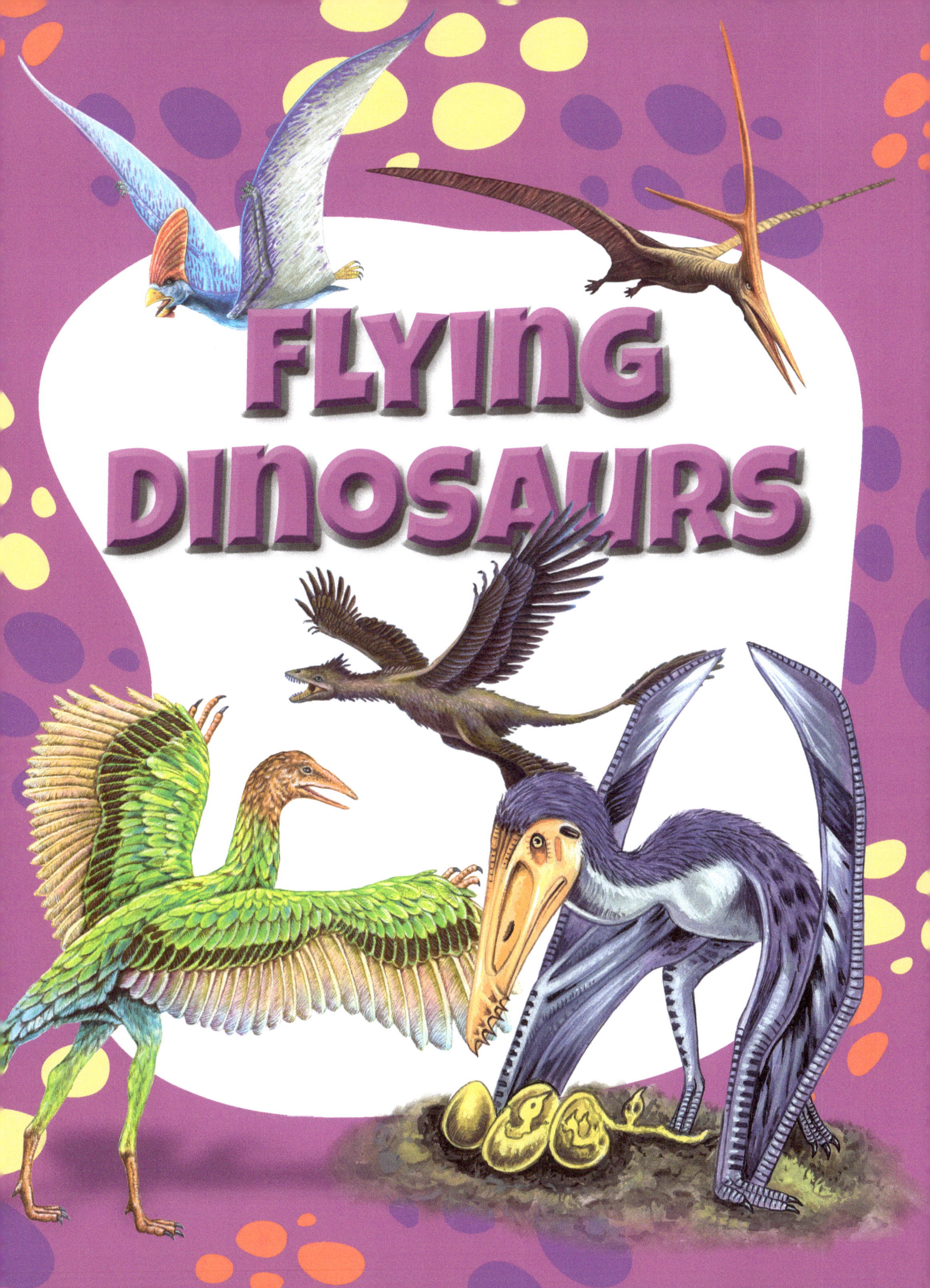

FLYING DINOSAURS

Flying Dinosaurs

Flying dinosaurs first appeared in the Late Triassic period and inhabited the skies until the end of the Cretaceous period. The theropods and other land-dwelling creatures gradually evolved into feathered dinosaurs, walking on their hind limbs. Over time, some large terrestrial dinosaurs became smaller in size, eventually developing wings and feathers. There is evidence that modern birds are descendants of dinosaurs, as both laid eggs and possessed features such as beaks and clawed feet, resembling birds.

Archaeopteryx

The Archaeopteryxes, meaning "ancient wings" or "first birds", were bird-like dinosaurs that acted as transitional species between dinosaurs and birds. They were among the earliest known avian species, dating back to the Late Jurassic period. Approximately the size of ravens, the Archaeopteryxes had broad wings, long tails, and small teeth, sharing many characteristics with theropod dinosaurs. Their feathers closely resembled those of modern birds, supporting the evolutionary link between non-avian dinosaurs and birds.

Archaeopteryx

Peteinosaurus

The Peteinosaurus were flying reptiles similar to pterosaurs that lived during the Late Triassic period. Fossils of these species were found in Europe. The name 'Petinosaurus' meant 'winged lizards', and these species existed around 210 million years ago. They had small wingspans and were smaller than other pterosaurs. Possessing elongated fingers, they preyed on dragonflies and other small insects. Their lightweight bones made them exceptionally fast and agile flyers.

Avisaurus

The Avisaurus, meaning 'bird lizard' belonged to the Late Cretaceous period. They were present in humid low-lying swamps, lakes and rivers. They lived alongside many giant dinosaurs. They lived around what is today the Rocky Mountains in North America. The best-known Avisaur is Angela.

Haopterus

The Haopterus, meaning "Haoxiao's wing", was a pterosaur native to China. With a slender, pointed snout with a rounded tip, its lower jaw measured approximately 128 mm in length. It possessed sharp, robust teeth. With a wingspan of about 5 feet and relatively weakly built hind limbs, this species existed during the Early Cretaceous period.

Haopterus

59

Confuciusornis

The Confuciusornis were crow-sized birds from the Early Cretaceous period, first discovered in China. They were among the earliest known beaked birds. Unlike the Archaeopteryxes, Confuciusornis lacked bony tails, indicating a shift towards a more modern bird-like skeletal structure. It was widely believed that primitive birds evolved from theropod dinosaurs, and the Confuciusornis represented a crucial stage in that transformation.

Microraptor

The Microraptors were small, four-winged dinosaurs that lived in what is now China. They were among the smallest known non-avian dinosaurs, measuring approximately 120 cm in length. The Microraptors had strong, well-developed feathers attached to their arms and legs, allowing them to glide between trees. They primarily fed on small animals, including fish. Fossils suggested they lived around 120 million years ago and had iridescent, glossy coats.

Dromaeosaurids

The Dromeosaurids were feathered theropods that lived during the Cretaceous period. They were medium-sized predators and had sickle-shaped claws on their inner toes. They were commonly referred to as raptors. They were covered in feathers and had large grasping hands. It was widely believed that Dromaeosaurids descended from Microraptors.

Dromaeosaurids

Rahonavis

The Rahonavis were bird-like theropods from the Late Cretaceous period, approximately 70 million years ago. They were small, predatory dinosaurs with sickle-shaped claws on their toes, resembling those of dromaeosaurs. About the size of ravens, Rahonavis lived in what is now Madagascar. Due to their many bird-like characteristics, some scientists initially classified them as primitive birds.

Laopteryx

The Laopteryx were pterosaurs that lived during the Late Jurassic period. Initially mistaken for birds, they were later confirmed to belong to the Pterosauria clade. The name 'Laopteryx' meant 'of venerable age', and they were among the oldest known pterosaurs discovered in the United States. Some scientists suggested they were closely related to the Archaeopterygidae, serving as a transitional link between dinosaurs and early birds. However, repeated revisions in classification regarding their species, gender, and true existence made their exact placement in the evolutionary tree uncertain.

Rahonavis

Top Pterosaurs

The Pterosaurs ranged in size from tiny species, comparable to sparrows, to giant species, the size of small planes. Pterosaurs were once considered primitive bird-like dinosaurs and were believed to be transitional species between birds and dinosaurs.

Anhanguera

The Anhanguera, meaning "old devils", had long, sharp-toothed jaws that were useful for catching small prey. They lived during the Early Cretaceous period. They were fish-eating reptiles with wingspans of about 1.5 metres (5 feet). They had angled, conical, curved teeth and tilted their heads upon landing to maintain proper balance.

Pteranodon

The Pteranodon, meaning 'toothless', had no teeth but possessed long crests on their heads, which helped counterbalance their weight. They lived during the Late Cretaceous period in what is now Kansas. They were primarily fish-eaters and had three-clawed fingers on each hand. They were aggressive and considered among the largest flying reptiles in history. Their wingspans reached nearly 10.7 metres (35 feet), and they primarily inhabited coastal regions.

Pteranodon

Ornithocheirus

The Ornithocheiruses, meaning 'bird hands', had fossils discovered in England. They were Pterosaurs that lived during the Late Cretaceous period. Their teeth were vertically aligned and angled outward. Pterosaurs were not direct ancestors of modern birds, but some species, such as Ornithocheiruses, had crests on their beaks, which were likely used as ornaments to attract mates.

Quetzalcoatlus

The Quetzalcoatli were giant flying reptiles named after the legendary feathered serpent god of Mexico. They lived during the Late Cretaceous period and were the largest known flying animals, with wingspans reaching 13.7 metres (45 feet). They were believed to have hunted fish and also scavenged for food. They fed similarly to modern skimmers and were known to inhabit swamps.

Rhamphorhynchus

The Rhamphorhynchuses were long-tailed Pterosaurs that lived during the Jurassic period. They had tails stiffened by ligaments and needle-like teeth. Their curved, sharp, and pointed beaks indicated a diet consisting primarily of fish.

Ornithocheirus

Largest Flying
Dinosaurs

The largest flying reptiles inhabited the land, seas, and skies. Some of these giant species dominated the skies. Their wingspans or neck lengths were often their most defining characteristics.

Coloborhynchus

The Coloborhynchuses were descendants of the Pterosaur family and lived during the Early Cretaceous period. They had two prominent front teeth that pointed forward and were used for tearing flesh from prey. The Coloborhynchuses were the largest toothed Pterosaurs ever discovered, with wingspans stretching up to seven metres wide.

Pelagornis

The Pelagornises were among the largest flying birds ever recorded. They lived approximately 25 million years ago and had wingspans of 6.5 metres, which were twice as long as those of the largest modern bird, the albatross. They were closely related to fowls, storks, and pelicans.

Coloborhynchus

Enantiornithes

The Enantiornithines were an extinct group of prehistoric birds that belonged to a broader dinosaur clade. They were not known to have left any descendants. Nearly 80 species were classified under this group, and some of them were discussed in this book.

Gobipteryx

The Gobipteryges were extinct birds from prehistoric times. They were not known to have any direct descendants. They were the first Enantiornithines ever discovered and were believed to have gone extinct at the end of the Cretaceous period. Their skulls measured 45 mm in length and were pointed. They had remarkable adaptations for flight and were capable of flying immediately after hatching.

Protopteryx

The Protopteryges were among the most basal Enantiornithines ever discovered. They were some of the most primitive birds of the Early Cretaceous period. Their feathers lacked the complex structures found in modern birds. Their long, thin tails were needle-like.

Small Cretaceous Dinosaurs

Caudipteryx

The Caudipteryges, meaning "tail feathers", were peacock-sized theropod dinosaurs that lived during the Early Cretaceous period. They were completely feathered and had bird-like appearances. Their slender legs indicated that they were swift runners. Some scientists classified the Caudipteryges as flightless birds, while others debated their exact classification.

Changyuraptor

Weighing approximately four kilograms (nine pounds) and measuring up to 1.2 metres (four feet) from head to tail, the Changyuraptors were large, four-winged predatory dinosaurs found in China. They were covered in feathers, including on their limbs, which gave them the appearance of having two pairs of wings. Their feathers and tails were among the longest, measuring up to 30 cm.

Anchiornis

The Anchiornises were chicken-sized dinosaurs covered in thick, long feathers. They were powerful runners and had black or grey plumage with red crests on their heads. The Anchiornises, meaning "near birds", were closely related to Archaeopteryxes.

Changyuraptor

Avimimus

The Avimimuses were parrot-beaked Oviraptosaurs with many bird-like features. Although some scientists debated their classification, they were generally not considered true birds. The Avimimuses served as evolutionary links between birds and dinosaurs. They stood approximately 70 cm tall and were fully feathered. The Avimimuses, meaning "amazing bird mimics", lived during the Cretaceous period.

Beipiaosaurus

The Beipiaosauruses lived in what is now China during the Early Cretaceous period. They were large, bizarre-looking therizinosaurs covered in shaggy, feather-like structures. They measured approximately two metres in height and had scythe-like claws. Although classified within the large carnivorous theropod family, their teeth suggested that they were herbivorous.

Dimorphodon

The Dimorphodons, meaning "two-form teeth", were flying reptiles that measured up to three metres and weighed around two kilograms. They were winged reptiles that walked on all fours. They had sharp talons suited for catching fish and lived during the Jurassic period.

Dimorphodon

Terrifying Flying
Reptiles

To see dinosaurs fly is a rather spectacular sight. The flying dinosaurs dominated the skies for thousands and thousands of years. The most famous group of flying reptiles were the Pterosaurs, which lived for more than 160 million years and evolved into the more complex birds of today.

Ikrandraco

The Ikrandracos were unique Pterosaurs with crests that unusually projected from their lower jaws. They also possessed head crests, which were not uncommon among Pterosaurs. Ikrandracos were the only flying reptiles known to have crests on their mandibles. They lived during the Early Cretaceous period, approximately 120 million years ago. It is believed that the small expandable pouches near their lower jaws helped them trap fish.

Nyctosaurus

The Nyctosauruses were known for their impressive head crests, which were massively forked and twice as large as their skulls. It is believed that the Nyctosauruses soared above the skies like modern-day albatrosses, hunting fish and other small mammals. Their wingspans reached about 2.7 metres (9 feet) in length.

Nyctosaurus

Nemicolopterus

The Nemicolopteruses provided evidence that not all Pterosaurs were giant flying reptiles, as they varied greatly in shape and size. The Nemicolopteruses were miniature Pterosaurs that only measured up to 25 cm from wing to wing, making them twice the size of modern hummingbirds. The Nemicolopteruses, meaning "hidden flying forest dwellers", had small curved toes that helped them grip tree branches. They fed on insects during the Early Cretaceous period.

Pterodactylus

The Pterodactyli were the first Pterosaurs ever discovered. They lived during the Jurassic period and were initially mistaken for sea creatures that swam across waters. With wingspans of about 1.5 metres (5 feet), they survived by feeding on fish and small creatures, which they grasped with their small-clawed feet. They had nearly 100 sharp teeth and were believed to have flown across the skies of what is now Germany. Their elongated fourth fingers on their forelimbs supported their wings during flight.

Pterodactylus

Sapeornis

The Sapeornises were a genus of birds that lived during the Early Cretaceous period. They displayed a mix of characteristics from the early Archaeopteryxes and more advanced bird forms that became prevalent during the Jurassic period. They lived during the Cretaceous period and had a small number of tail flight feathers. The Sapeornises had small teeth capable of chewing on insects. They were known for swallowing stones to aid digestion. The Sapeornises were only active during daylight hours.

Omnivoropteryx

The Omnivoropteryxes, meaning "omnivorous wings", were primitive flying creatures that lived during the Cretaceous period. Scientists claimed that they were closely related to the Sapeornises. They were found flying across the skies of what is now China. Their wings were long enough to suggest that they did not need to run or jump to take off into flight. They had short legs that were used for perching on branches. They were opportunistic omnivores, meaning they fed on plants and seeds but also hunted insects and small mammals from time to time. They were early birds that acted as active predators.

Sapeornis

Argentavis

The Argentavises, meaning "magnificent silver birds", were one of the largest flying birds ever discovered. They lived during the Cretaceous period and inhabited what is now Argentina. Their humeri were only slightly smaller than human arms. They had stout, strong legs with large feet that enabled them to walk sturdily on the ground. Their wingspans reached 6 metres (20 feet), and they were considered land birds, primarily feeding on small terrestrial animals and insects. Research suggests that they swallowed their prey whole rather than tearing flesh from them.

Tapejara wellnhoferi

The Tapejaras were a marvel to watch in the skies, as they were Brazilian Pterosaurs that lived during the Early Cretaceous period. They had semi-circular crests mounted over their snouts and a bony structure on their heads. They were carnivorous flying reptiles that preyed on small creatures and scavenged dead animals. With wingspans of 1.4 metres (4.6 feet), they weighed only 400 grams and could reach speeds of about 29 km/h (18 mph).

Tapejara

Hatzegopteryx

The Hatzegopteryges were among the largest flying reptiles to have ever existed. Their skulls measured nearly 3 metres in length, and their wingspans reached about 10 metres. They fed on small creatures, picking up prey with their long beaks. These Pterosaurs were of gigantic proportions and stood at a height of 6 metres. Their heavily built skulls contrasted sharply with the lightweight skulls of other Pterosaurs. They inhabited Europe around 65 million years ago. The Hatzegopteryges were considered the largest and the last of the Pterosaurs.

Herbstosaurus

The Herbstosauruses were Pterosaurs that lived during the Jurassic period. They inhabited what is now South America and were classified as flying reptiles. They were originally described as small dinosaurs. The Herbstosauruses, meaning "Herbst Lizards", were initially assumed to be Theropod dinosaurs but were later reclassified as flying reptiles.

Hatzegopteryx

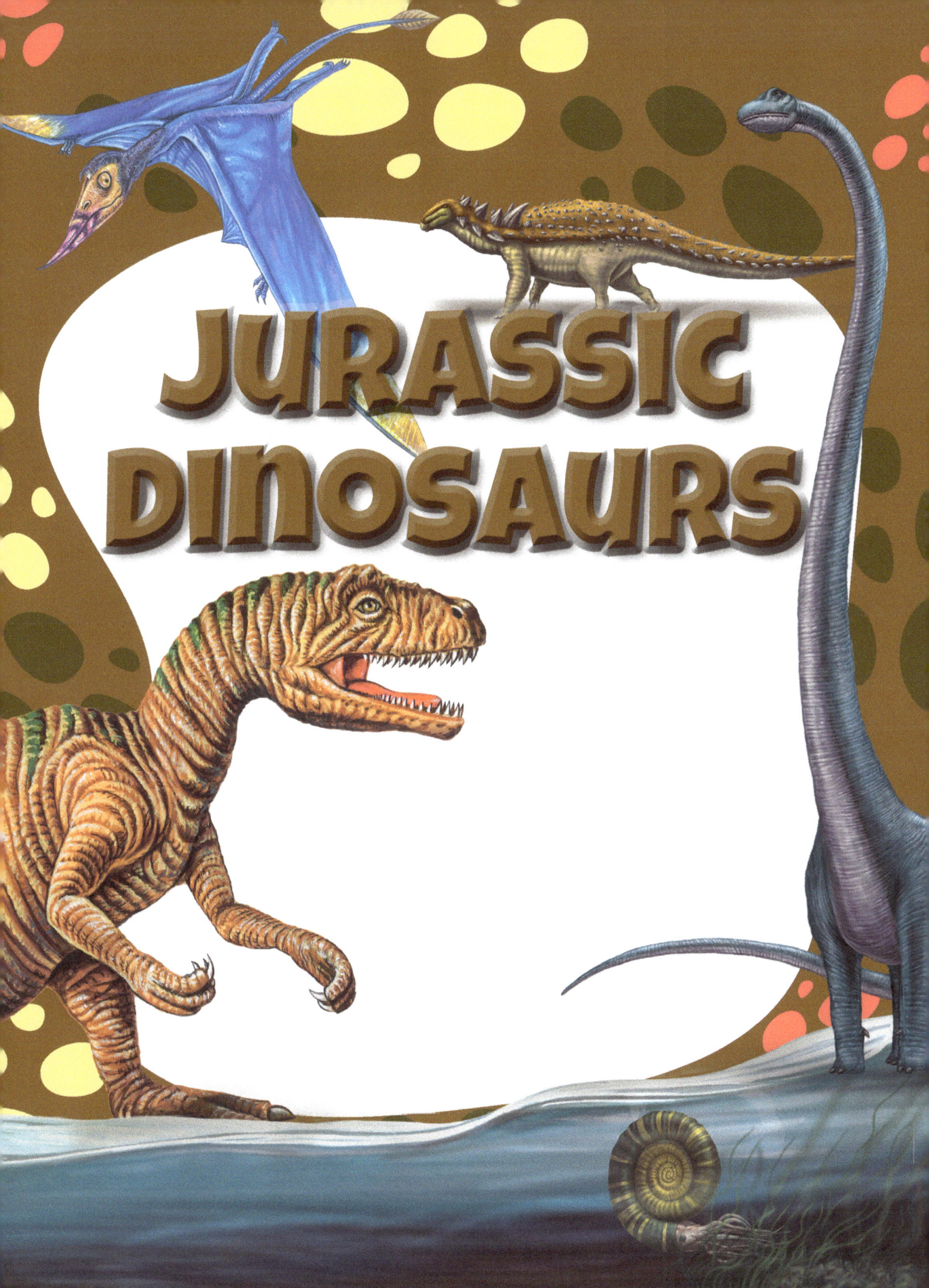

JURASSIC DINOSAURS

Jurassic Dinosaurs

The Jurassic period occurred in the second segment of the Mesozoic era, following the Triassic period, and lasted for 56 million years. Although the mass extinction before the Jurassic period wiped out many species, some dinosaurs survived and entered the Jurassic period.

Stegosaurus

The Stegosauruses were among the most common dinosaurs of the Jurassic period. With 17 bony spines extending along their backs, these unique dinosaurs existed 150 million years ago. They had powerful spiked tails and weighed up to 5 tonnes. The Stegosauruses, meaning "roofed lizards", swallowed rocks to aid digestion. They were herbivores with some of the smallest brains and were extremely slow-moving dinosaurs.

Brachiosaurus

The Brachiosauruses were famous for their long necks and massive structures. They lived during the Mid-Jurassic period and had giraffe-like appearances. The Brachiosauruses, meaning "arm lizards", had longer forelimbs than hindlimbs. They were completely herbivorous and warm-blooded. They belonged to a group of sauropods called Gigantotherms due to their enormous size.

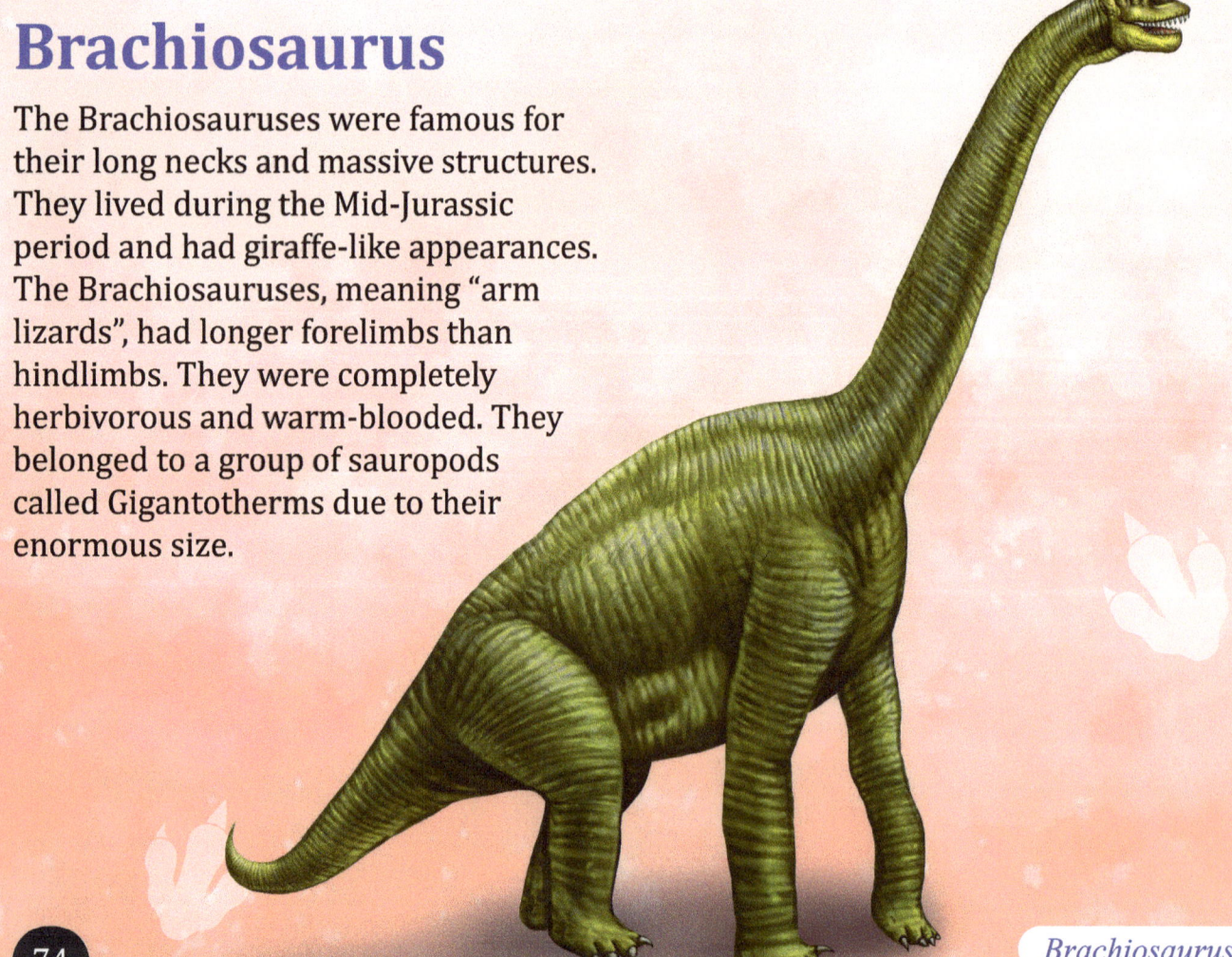

Brachiosaurus

Camptosaurus

The Camptosauruses were beaked herbivores of the Late Jurassic period. They lived around 155 million years ago and were typical Iguanodontids, moving from one place to another in search of plants. The Camptosauruses had long tails for counterbalance, and their forelimbs were used to fend off predators. They measured about 6 metres (20 feet) in length and primarily walked on all fours.

Scelidosaurus

The Scelidosaurus was a plant-eating dinosaur of the Early Jurassic period. The Scelidosaurus was named by the same person who coined the word 'dinosaur', Mr. Richard Owen. These dinosaurs had small rounded stubs on their skin. They were classified as 'bird-hipped' dinosaurs and were one of the most heavily armoured species.

Supersaurus

The Supersauruses were huge herbivores with tremendously elongated necks and whip-like tails. They grew as large as 40 metres (130 feet) and swallowed food whole rather than chewing. Their teeth were effective in scraping vegetation from trees. They were one of the longest sauropods of the Jurassic period but not the heaviest.

Supersaurus

Shastasaurus

The Shastasauruses were marine reptiles that survived from the Triassic period into the Jurassic period. They were a type of Ichthyosaur named after Mount Shasta. They measured up to 21 metres (69 feet) in length and were among the largest marine reptiles ever known. Their large size enabled them to take in significant amounts of air and hold their breath while diving deep into the ocean.

Plesiosaurs

The Plesiosaurs were predatory marine reptiles and were among the first of their group to be discovered. They had no protective armour and were an easy prey for other marine predators. They gave birth to live young like modern sea turtles and had four wide, paddle-like flippers used to swim across waters. They had a long necks and a tapered body. Their wide jaws and teeth were effective enough to catch prey in the seas.

Stenopterygius

The Stenopterygiuses were Ichthyosaur reptiles that lived during the Jurassic period and resembled tuna fish. They fed on small marine animals and were present around 180 million years ago. Their lifestyles were similar to modern-day dolphins. The Stenopterygiuses, meaning "narrow fins", grew up to 4 metres (13 feet) in length and weighed about 90 kilograms (200 pounds). They had dominant dorsal fins for steering.

Plesiosaurs

The evolution of birds began in the Jurassic period. Most of the birds were believed to have evolved from the clade Theropoda and the earliest of birds belong to the clade Paraves. These birds survived many mass extinctions, giving rise to our modern birds, namely the ostriches, ducks and fowl.

Archaeopteryx

The Archaeopteryx, meaning the 'original bird' was one of the first bird-like forms to have evolved from reptiles. They were non-avian feathered dinosaurs. They had long Velociraptor claws that enabled them to catch prey easily. The growth rate of their siblings was so slow that some of them grew up to the size of a kiwi and then proceeded to gradually increase. They had bird-like brains and were known as the missing link between birds and dinosaurs.

Rhamphorhynchus

They were long-tailed pterosaurs found in the Jurassic period. The Rhamphorhynchus had a beak snout and a wingspan of up to 5.75 feet. They were the size of a rock pigeon. They were the earliest known pterosaur and were known for having an extremely stable flight, a feature that is found in bats and dragonflies. They were about 20 inches long and weighed about a pound or two.

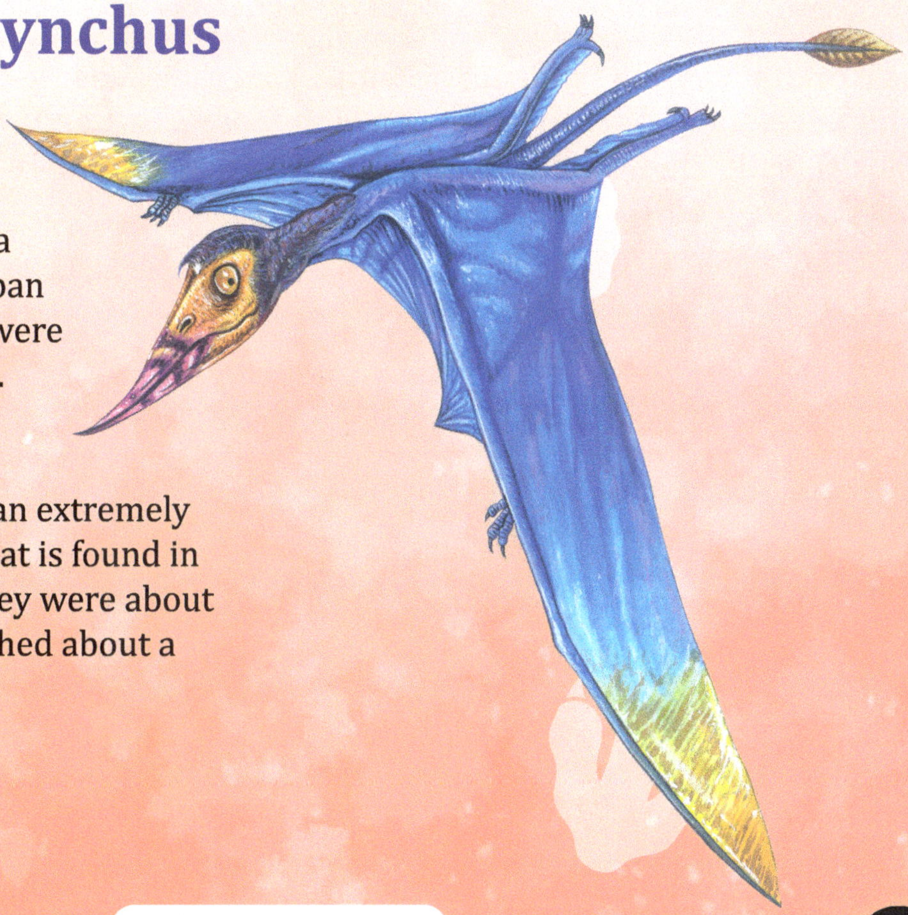

Rhamphorhynchus

Early Jurassic
Dinosaurs

Scutellosaurus

The Scutellosaurus was found 200 million years ago, in the Early Jurassic period. They were characterised by small thorns or scutes found on their back and the sides. They belonged to the armoured dinosaur group and resembled modern day lizards. The Scutellosaurus had very powerful hindlegs that enabled to run very fast, to save itself from ferocious predators. They were believed to be plant-eaters.

Abrictosaurus

The Abrictosauruses were small dinosaurs initially thought to be omnivores but possibly herbivores. They weighed less than 45 kilograms (99 pounds) and grew up to 1.5 metres (5 feet) in length. The Abrictosauruses, meaning "wakeful lizards", lived around 199 million years ago. Scientists found that the Abrictosauruses were closely related to the Heterodontosauruses due to their similar tooth structures.

Heterodontosaurus

The Heterodontosaur belonged to the ornithischian order. They were considered as basal ornithopods and weighed around 6 kilograms. The Heterdontosaur, meaning 'different teeth lizard' had biting capabilities of tearing and grinding due to its three kinds of teeth. They were found 200 million years ago. These dinosaurs had a cheek area to store food, the way some modern day mammals do.

Heterodontosaur

The Brown
Jurassic

The Brown Jurassic period is also called the Middle Jurassic period and ended about 163 million years. In the mid- Jurassic period, the supercontinent Pangea started to split further apart.

Damalasaurus

The Damalasauruses, meaning "Damala lizards", were sauropods that lived during the Mid-Jurassic period. They were herbivorous dinosaurs classified under the Sauropod family. The Damalasauruses were found in Tibet. Although classified as basal sauropods, they have never been formally described, leaving many details about them a mystery.

Sarcolestes

The Sarcolesteses, meaning "flesh robbers", were classified under a group of Ankylosaurian dinosaurs. Unfortunately, only lower jawbones of these dinosaurs were discovered, so limited information is available about them. However, it is known that they were herbivores.

Amygdalodon

The Amygdalodons were herbivorous dinosaurs with long necks that inhabited South America. Their hind legs were longer than their forelimbs. They mainly fed on low-lying vegetation.

Sarcolestes

Barosaurus

The Barosauruses were giant, long-tailed, long-necked herbivores that lived during the Late Jurassic period. They were closely related to the Diplodocuses. Measuring over 26 metres (85 feet) in length and weighing approximately 100 tonnes, the Barosauruses, meaning "heavy lizards", were among the largest known dinosaurs. Their extremely long necks, which measured up to 17 metres (56 feet), were hollow and lightweight, allowing them to move their necks easily while grazing on vegetation.

Kentrosaurus

The Kentrosauruses were large herbivores covered in extensive armour, measuring approximately 5 metres (17 feet) from snout to tail. The Kentrosauruses, meaning "spiked lizards", had numerous cheek teeth that helped in chewing vegetation efficiently. Their brains were the size of walnuts, and they likely consumed up to 136 kilograms (300 pounds) of food per day for survival.

Dryosaurus

The Dryosauruses, meaning "tree lizards", were extremely fast, horny-beaked Iguanodonts. They were also called "high oak lizards" because of their oak-shaped cheek teeth. They had five fingers on each hand, long stiff tails, and long, slender legs. These dinosaurs were herbivores and moved in herds. They used their tails for counterbalance and to defend themselves against predators.

Barosaurus

Jurassic Vegetation

The Jurassic vegetation mainly consisted of seed ferns, horsetails, conifers and gingkoes. The Jurassic period was also called the "Age of Cycads" due to the abundance of the cycad plants.

Cycads

The Cycads were diverse during the Jurassic period. These seed-bearing, palm-like plants grew as tall as trees. The Sauropods and other herbivores depended on cycads as a primary food source. Some cycads were short and stubby, making them accessible to smaller herbivores. The Cycads were often referred to as 'Dinosaur Plants'. They have a long fossil history and have existed since the age of dinosaurs.

Hadrosaurs

The evolution of cycads declined when the Hadrosauruses became dominant after the Jurassic period. These herbivorous dinosaurs had enormous banks of shearing teeth that allowed them to chew tough vegetation. Since they relied on other food sources rather than cycad seeds, cycad populations declined significantly, leading to reduced seed dispersion.

Hadrosaurs

Diversity of Dinosaurs

The Jurassic period is known for a significant increase in the diversity of dinosaurs. During the Early Jurassic period, small, lightly boned theropods evolved as insectivores. By the end of the period, massive predators like Allosauruses and Ceratosauruses had evolved, along with large Sauropods like the Brachiosauruses.

Dilophosaurus

The Dilophosauruses were among the largest known carnivores of the Early Jurassic period. They relied on scent as a hunting technique. They had long, slender, rear-curving teeth designed for gripping and tearing flesh from prey. Their long tails may have been used as whips during fights with other dinosaurs. They had frills and venom glands, which allowed them to spit venom up to 6 metres (20 feet) to defend against predators.

Ceratosaurus

The Ceratosauruses, meaning "horned lizards", were enormous theropod dinosaurs that lived during the Late Jurassic period. They had blade-like horns on their snouts and pairs of hornlets above their eyes. These large carnivores were bipedal and had sharp, serrated teeth. They weighed around 980 kilograms (2,160 pounds) and reached up to 6 metres (20 feet) in length. Scientists believed that the large nasal horns of young Ceratosauruses may have helped them hatch from their eggs.

Ceratosaurus

Shelled Molluscs

The Ammonites evolved from the Early Jurassic period and existed through a time interval of 140 million years. The Ammonites became extinct at the same time as dinosaurs. During the Jurassic period, the ammonites evolved as shelled animals and had protective shells around their bodies. They were marine animals and fed on small planktons and vegetation that grew on the sea floor.

Pavlovia

The Pavlovias were an extinct group of ammonites that lived during the Late Jurassic period. They were fast-moving nektonic carnivores with shells reaching diameters of about 40 millimetres. They had complicated suture lines that were completely fastened to the shell walls.

Stephanoceras

The Stephanoceras, meaning 'crown horn', lived during the mid-Jurassic period. They had shells with well-developed ribbing and tubercles. They were a sandstone colour and had features that distinguished between male and female molluscs.

Ammonites

Teleosauridae

The Teleosaurids were a group of marine crocodyliforms that lived during the Jurassic period. They had elongated jaws, sharp teeth, and short but powerful forelimbs, and they were similar to modern-day Gharials. Their brown, scaly skin and back spikes gave them a fearsome appearance. They also had large horns at the back of their heads.

Metriorhynchids

The Metriorhynchids were an extinct group of marine crocodyliforms that lived in the Jurassic oceans. The Metriorhynchuses, found during the Mid-Jurassic period, measured about 3 metres (10 feet) in length, making them shorter than many modern crocodiles. They were versatile hunters, preying on slow-moving ammonites as well as faster, larger prey such as Pterosaurs. Unlike their land-dwelling relatives, the Metriorhynchuses lost most of their body armour to improve swimming speed, a feature similar to modern dolphins.

Rudist

Rudists were tube or ring shaped bivalves that evolved during the Later Jurassic period. They formed a major part of the reef on the sea floors. They were elongated and called true reef-builders of the Jurassic period.

Metriorhynchidae

Australochelys

The Australochelyses were primitive turtles from the Early Jurassic period. Fossils of these ancient turtles were found in South Africa, making them the most ancient known African turtles. They were one of the first turtles to develop hard shells, offering protection against predators.

Condorchelys

The Condorchelyses were turtles that lived during the Jurassic period in South America. Since only partial remains of these turtles were uncovered, details about their diet and habitat remain uncertain. They were a genus of stem turtles. They inhabited the Jurassic oceans about 183 million years ago. Their fossils revealed that they had no teeth, and their discovery provided insight into turtle evolution during the Mid-Jurassic period.

Eileanchelys

The Eileanchelyses were primitive turtles that lived during the Mid-Jurassic period, approximately 164 million years ago. They were among the earliest known swimming turtles. Their fossils suggested that they were pond turtles, forming an evolutionary link between land and sea turtles. These light, aquatic creatures had fragile shells measuring around 30 cm (12 inches) in length.

Eileanchelys

Steven Spielberg's "Jurassic Park"

The Jurassic Park was a thriller movie directed by Steven Spielberg, that released in the year 1993. The movie featured a wildlife park where a group of enthusiasts set out on a joyride, only to discover the danger of carnivores and other predators in the Jurassic period, from whom they managed to escape and survive. This movie was inspired by the Jurassic period and many dinosaurs featured in the film. The movie starred famous dinosaurs like the Tyrannosaurus Rex, Dilophosaurus, Velociraptors, Brachiosaurs and Triceratops. Other dinosaurs that appeared are described below.

Gallimimus

The Gallimimuses were ornithopod dinosaurs that could grow up to 8 metres (26 feet) in length. Known as one of the largest and fastest theropods of their time, they were believed to have moved in packs. The Gallimimuses, meaning "chicken mimics", were featured in Jurassic Park and were primarily insectivores, occasionally feeding on plant seeds, fruits, and even dinosaur eggs.

Parasaurolophus

The Parasaurolophus, meaning 'near crested lizard' were herbivorous that was both a biped and a quadruped. They were large duck-billed dinosaurs that had an elongated tube-like projection on their heads, which were used to emit signals to other dinosaurs. They weighed around 3 tons and measured up to 10 metres in length.

Parasaurolophus

End of
Jurassic Period

The end of the Jurassic period saw many extinctions, even though this extinction was pretty minor. Around 80% of the marine bivalves vanished, but gave way to newer species that evolved in the next geological period. Some of the dinosaurs that completely vanished, were the Tuojiangosaurus, Mamenchisaurus and others.

Mamenchisaurus

They were found in the Late Jurassic period and were known for their remarkably long necks. They were found living 145 million years ago and were known as one of the largest species, reaching 35 metres in length, weighing around 75 tonnes. The Mamenchisaurs drank around 900 litres (200 gallons) of water and ate tons of plants to keep them going throughout the day.

Tuojiangosaurus

The Tuojiangosauruses were herbivorous stegosaurian dinosaurs from the Late Jurassic period. These dinosaurs had plates and spikes protruding from their backs, which were embedded in their skin rather than their skeletons. They had four large spikes at the ends of their tails, which were used for defence against predators. Their arched backs, small heads, longer hind legs, and shorter forelimbs distinguished them from other stegosaurians.

Mamenchisaurus

Prominent
Dinosaurs

Although many species of dinosaurs existed during the Jurassic period, some dinosaurs continued to dominate others. Some dinosaurs such as the Allosauruses and the Diplodocuses, were very prominent during this period and were famous during the Jurassic times.

Allosaurus

The Allosaurs, meaning 'different lizard', lived during the Late Jurassic period. They were massive carnivores that grew up to 35 feet in length and 15 feet in height. Their mouths contained dozens of sharp teeth that helped tear into flesh easily. They were one of the most fearsome carnivores that had two powerful hind limbs and a large tail. They mostly fed on large herbivore dinosaurs, and possibly scavenged other dinosaurs' meals as well.

Diplodocus

The Diplodocuses were enormous sauropod dinosaurs that grew up to 30 metres (100 feet) in length. Their elongated necks accounted for a significant portion of their body length, allowing them to graze across vast areas of vegetation. These gentle giants travelled in herds, much like modern elephants, and weighed approximately 11 tonnes, equivalent to their near cousin, the Brachiosaurus.

Allosaurus

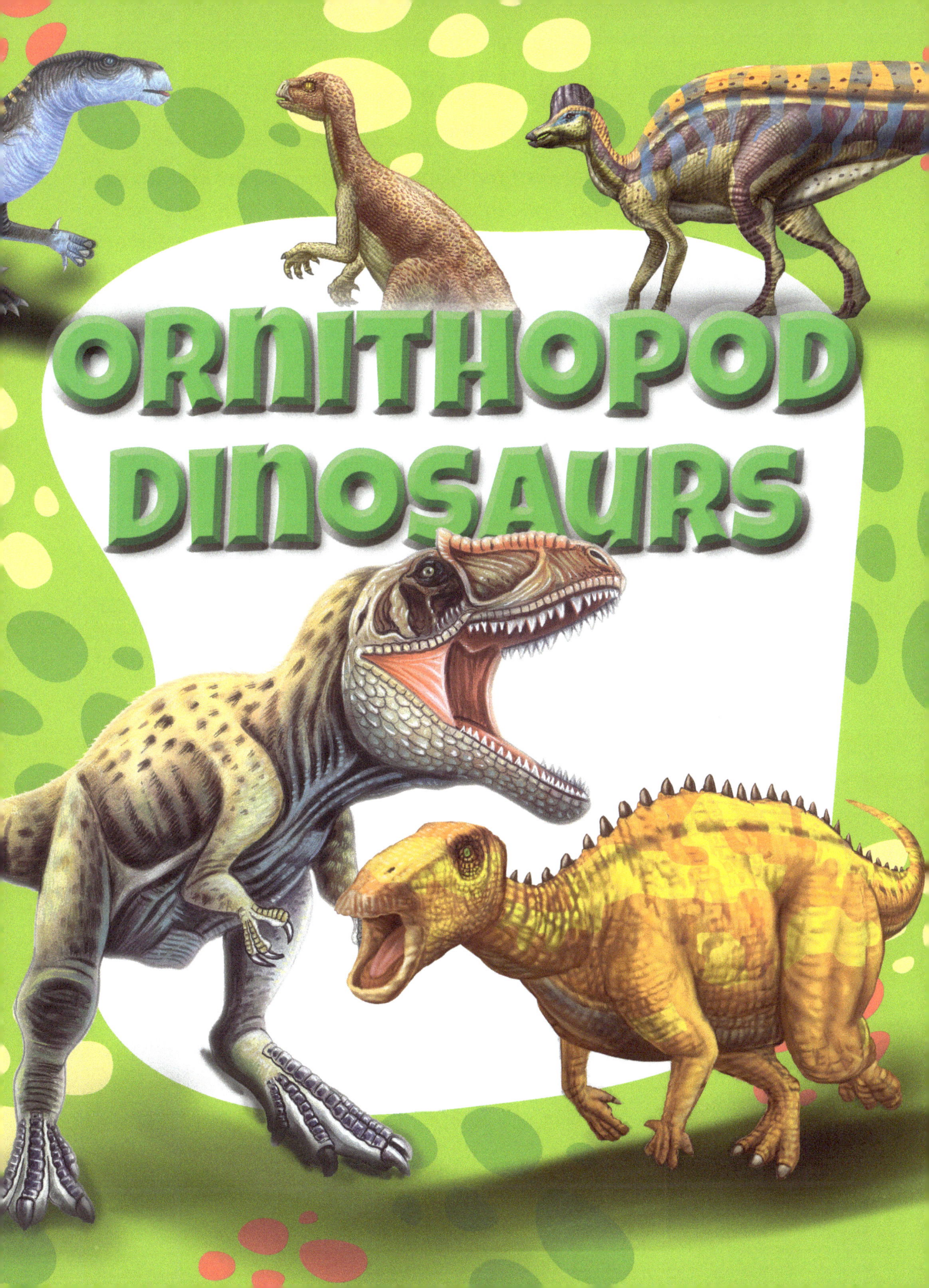

ORNITHOPOD DINOSAURS

Ornithopod
Dinosaurs

Ornithopod dinosaurs were bird-hipped dinosaurs that had three-toed feet. They had no armour, a horny beak and some had thin cartilaginous plates along the outside of their ribs. They were the most successful herbivores during the Cretaceous period. They were small, bipedal creatures that grew into large herbivores later during the Late Cretaceous period. All Ornithopods had a pelvis bone pointing backwards.

Iguanodon

The most important Ornithopod dinosaurs were the Iguanodons. They were 9 metres long and 2 metres tall. They weighed around 5 tonnes. The Iguanodons derived their name from the Iguanas since both had similar teeth. They lived from the Late Jurassic to the Early Cretaceous period, and the joints of these dinosaurs were very flexible.

Parasaurolophus

The Parasaurolophus, meaning "beside/near crested lizard" weighed about 3.5 tonnes and was a large herbivorous dinosaur. It was a very interesting dinosaur, having a strange shaped head that had a curved crest. Scientists believed that this crest helped regulate body temperature. They lived in the Late Cretaceous period.

Iguanodon

Hadrosaurs

The Hadrosaurs were a family of ornithopod dinosaurs. They were further divided into two sub families - Lambeosaurines and Saurolophines. They were a group of duck-billed dinosaurs with flat, long, duck-like snouts and toothless beaks.

Lambeosaurus

The Lambeosaurus belonged to the sub family Lambeosaurinae and they were noted for having hollow, bony crests. Their crests were hatchet-shaped, with a blade pointing upwards, and the handle pointing backwards. Scientists believe that this crest must have been used to emit signals as a form of communication with other dinosaurs. They were about 10 metres long and 3 metres tall.

Edmontosaurus

Although the Edmontosauruses did not resemble all other hadrosaurs, they had small soft-tissue crests that were only mildly visible over their heads. They belonged to the Saurolophine family, in which the dinosaurs lacked head crests. However, the Edmontosauruses still had head ornaments and grew up to 13 metres long. They were actively preyed upon by large Theropods such as T. rexes.

Edmontosaurus

Hypacrosaurus

The Hypacrosaurus belonged to the Hadrosaur family and lived during the Cretaceous period. The snouts of the Hypacrosauruses featured toothless bills at the front with rows of self-sharpening teeth at the back. Like all other duck-billed dinosaurs, the Hypacrosauruses had hollow crests on top of their heads, which were used to make loud horn blasts that could be heard from a distance. The Hypacrosauruses, meaning "near highest lizards," were given their name because they were the second-largest hadrosaurs next to the Shantungosauruses.

Shantungosaurs

The Shantungosauruses were the largest hadrosaurs to have ever walked the Earth. In fact, they were the largest known Ornithopods to have lived on this planet. They did not have any notable head display features but had large nostril openings. This may have been due to their large body masses requiring a high intake of oxygen.

Maiasaura

Maiasaura, meaning 'good mother lizard,' laid its eggs in large nesting colonies and is believed to have nurtured its young. It provided the first clear evidence that hadrosaurs took the time and effort to care for their offspring before they were ready to leave the nest. Maiasaura was a large, herbivorous ornithopod that lived during the Late Cretaceous period.

Saurolophus

The Saurolophuses were known to have small or nearly invisible bony head crests. They belonged to the Saurolophine subfamily and lived 70 million years ago. Scientists once believed that the Saurolophuses were semi-aquatic animals, using their head crests as snorkels for breathing while submerged. However, more recent studies suggest that they were more likely used for making loud resonating calls, making them some of the noisiest dinosaurs on the planet. Some palaeontologists theorise that the Saurolophuses might have inflated air sacs like balloons at times to attract mates.

Gryposaurus

Gryposaurus, meaning 'hook-nosed lizard,' had a large nasal display but no head crest. It was a large duck-billed dinosaur that lived around 84 million years ago during the Late Cretaceous period. It grew up to 40 feet long and weighed approximately 5 tons. Its distinctive nasal bump likely played a role in vocalizations, allowing it to honk and blare at other herd members or signal potential threats, such as large predators like Tyrannosaurus rex and raptors.

Gryposaurus

Polar Ornithopods

The ornithopod dinosaurs are believed to have been distributed across all the continents of the world, mostly Asia, except for Antarctica. Only two species of dinosaurs were present in the near Antarctic Australia region and had unusually large eyes which were assumed to have been used against limited sunlight.

Leaellynasaura

One remarkable fact about Leaellynasaura is that they were polar dinosaurs, adapted to extreme seasonal conditions. They faced challenges surviving through cycles of freezing winters and seasonal thaws. Their tails were exceptionally long, comprising almost 75 per cent of their total body length. They are believed to have been covered in light brown proto-feathers, providing insulation against the cold. Leaellynasaura are among the most well-known dinosaurs from Australia.

Qantassaurus

Qantassaurus were small, bipedal, herbivorous ornithopods that lived near the Antarctic Circle during the Early Cretaceous period. Weighing around 45 kilograms and growing up to six feet long, they were agile runners resembling small, grey kangaroos. Their large eyes likely helped them see in dim polar light. Thought to be endothermic, they could sustain activity in cold environments. Environmental changes may have led to their decline rather than melting ice.

Leaellynasaura

Humped Dinosaurs

Some dinosaurs of the Ornithoschian family had camel-like humps on their backs, apart from their distinguishing duck-billed feature. The Morelladon and Ouranosaurus were sail-backed dinosaurs that fall under the category of ornithopod dinosaurs.

Ouranosaurus

Ouranosaurus, meaning "brave lizards," lived in North Africa during the Early Cretaceous period. They measured approximately 8 metres in length and had distinctive sails or camel-like humps on their backs, reaching about two feet in height. These structures are believed to have played a role in thermoregulation, helping them absorb or dissipate heat depending on the climate. Ouranosaurus had high-placed nostrils, an adaptation that may have facilitated swimming across rivers while they foraged on low-growing vegetation.

Morelladon

Morelladon were an extinct genus of ornithopod dinosaurs from the Early Cretaceous period in present-day Spain. Growing up to six metres long, they had distinctive sail-like humps formed by elongated neural spines. These structures likely helped regulate body temperature. As herbivores, they stood out among ornithopods due to their unique adaptations for environmental regulation, making them a fascinating discovery in dinosaur evolution.

Ouranosaurus

Heaviest
Ornithopods

Ornithopods were generally medium-sized herbivores until the emergence of enormous genera of dinosaurs during the mid-Cretaceous period. They originated in Asia and Africa, weighing approximately 5 to 6 tonnes. Later, larger ornithopods evolved during the Late Cretaceous period. Some of the heaviest known ornithopods included Lanzhousaurus and Lurdusaurus.

Lanzhousaurus

Lanzhousaurus was an exceptionally large ornithopod and is recognised as one of the largest herbivorous dinosaurs. They possessed unusually large teeth in their lower jaws, which remains a subject of scientific debate. Although Lanzhousaurus was a herbivore, the presence of such large teeth suggests an unknown adaptation, possibly related to its diet or feeding behaviour.

Lurdusaurus

Lurdusauruses were once believed to be semi-aquatic dinosaurs and were popularly known as the river dinosaurs of the Sahara. They were herbivores that lived during the Early Cretaceous period. Their body structure suggests that they may have been adapted to a slightly different lifestyle compared to other ornithopods. They likely spent much of their time in water, using their long necks to reach underwater plants. The environment during the Cretaceous period is thought to have been dominated by rivers, seas, lakes, and marshes.

Lanzhousaurus

Feathered
Ornithopods

Ornithopods were mainly famous for their duck-billed group of dinosaurs. But some ornithopods evolved into feathered dinosaurs. For example, the Tianyulong and Kulindadromeus.

Tianyulong

Tianyulongs were small, fuzzy, feathered ornithischian dinosaurs. What makes Tianyulongs unique is that they are considered distant relatives of all feathered dinosaurs. Unlike most feathered dinosaurs, which were theropods, Tianyulongs were ornithischians, making them evolutionary outliers. Despite being ornithopods, which typically had duck-billed features, Tianyulongs possessed primitive filament-like structures, suggesting that feathers may have been more widespread among dinosaurs than previously thought.

Kulindadromeus

Kulindadromeuses were feathered, herbivorous dinosaurs that lived near lakes and lowlands during the Jurassic period. Previously, it was believed that only carnivorous dinosaurs had feathers, but Kulindadromeuses provided the first evidence of feather-like structures in ornithischians. They had simple bristles, which evolved into more complex feathers over time. Measuring only one metre in length, they had short snouts, indicating adaptations to low-lying vegetation.

Kulindadromeus

Primitive
Dinosaurs

Ornithopods were usually considered medium-sized, well-developed dinosaurs, classified into families and subfamilies based on their duck-billed features and other unique characteristics. However, some of the more primitive ornithopods were smaller in size and less evolved compared to their later relatives.

Fabrosaurus

Fabrosauruses were small dinosaurs that resembled modern toy breed dogs in size. They lived during the Early Jurassic period in the Mesozoic era. As primitive ornithopods, Fabrosauruses were herbivores that primarily fed on ferns and other low-growing vegetation. They lived in Africa approximately 200 million years ago. Their hip structure bore a strong resemblance to that of modern birds.

Lesothosaurus

Lesothosaurus bore a striking resemblance to Fabrosaurus. They coexisted with Fabrosaurus approximately 200 million years ago in South Africa. These two species shared similar feeding habits and physical traits. Similar to that of modern-day gazelles, they were agile herbivores that grew up to 3 metres in length. Lesothosaurus had an elongated body and a three-foot-long tail. The name "Lesothosaurus" means "Lesotho," referencing their lizard-like appearance.

Lesothosaurus

Horny-Beaked
Ornithopods

Ornithopods were lightly built herbivores who were either duck-billed snout or small horns protruding from their heads. Some ornithopods had horny beaks that resembled those of modern day birds. Some examples of horny beaked dinosaurs are Heterodontosaurs, Brachylophosaurus and Hypsilophodon.

Heterodontosaurus

Heterodontosauruses were small, beaked, plant-eating dinosaurs that lived during the Early Jurassic period. They had three distinct types of teeth, which enabled them to process a variety of plant materials efficiently. They stored food in their cheek pouches and possessed five-fingered hands and stiff, elongated tails. Roughly the size of turkeys, they weighed about 42 pounds (approximately 19 kilograms). Heterodontosauruses were relatively fast-moving ornithopods.

Brachylophosaurus

Brachylophosauruses, meaning "short-crested lizards," were mid-sized herbivorous, duck-billed dinosaurs from the Late Cretaceous period. As typical hadrosaurs, they possessed beak-like mouths. Their elongated heads featured upper beaks that widened towards the edge, which may have assisted in gathering and processing vegetation.

Brachylophosaurus

Fast Runners

Ornithopod dinosaurs ranged from small, bipedal species to large, herbivorous ones. The smaller, turkey-sized ornithopods were typically equipped with long, slender legs useful for fast running. All ornithopods were herbivorous, and only some fed on insects.

Xiaosaurus

Xiaosauruses were small, herbivorous ornithopods that lived during the mid-Jurassic period, about 170 million years ago. They were bipedal, walking on two long legs with four-toed feet. The name Xiaosaurus, meaning "dawn lizard," reflects their early place in ornithopod evolution. With five-fingered hands and lizard-like traits, these rare ornithischians were exceptionally fast runners.

Oryctodromeus

The Oryctodromeus, meaning 'digging runner' were small ornithopod dinosaurs that lived during the mid-Cretaceous period. They exhibited a strange burrowing behaviour and scientists found that they dug underground making a den or burrow to live in. It is assumed that small dinosaurs shared this burrow to protect themselves from large predators as well as to weather the harsh climatic conditions.

Xiaosaurus

Orodromeus

The 'Mountain Runner,' Orodromeus, is one of the most spectacular dinosaurs ever discovered from the Late Cretaceous. Fossils provide insights into its nests, eggs, hatchlings, juveniles, adults, growth, and habitat, though much remains unknown. The mother likely laid around 12 eggs. With simple, leaf-shaped teeth for a plant-based diet and insects, Orodromeus was a long-legged Ornithopod, relying on speed to escape predators.

Hypsilophodon

Hypsilophodon was a small ornithopod dinosaur that measured around five feet in length and weighed approximately 50 pounds. Its name was derived from its distinctive teeth, which were well-suited for processing plant material. This dinosaur possessed long, slender legs adapted for fast running. It had a stiff, elongated tail that provided balance while in motion. A herbivore, Hypsilophodon relied on its agility and swift legs to evade larger carnivorous predators.

Valdosaurus

Valdosauruses were similar to Hypsilophodons in both features and adaptations. They lived during the Early Cretaceous period and were herbivorous, bipedal dinosaurs. These "forest lizards" belonged to the Iguanodontian ornithopods.

Hypsilophodon

Ornithopod
Footprints

A lot of confusion has arisen between the footprints of a large bipedal herbivorous dinosaur and a carnivorous dinosaur. Scientists have felt that differentiating between the footprints of a meat-eating dinosaur and a plant-eating dinosaur is quite a challenging task.

Theropod Footprints

Tracks made by Theropods have sizeable claw marks at the ends of their toes. The toe prints appear quite slender, and the footprint is longer than it is wide. When the length is compared to the width, the footprint forms a distinctive "V" shape

Ornithopod Footprints

The well-preserved footprint tracks of herbivorous Ornithopod dinosaurs lack distinctive claw marks. The ends of the toes were more blunt and round-shaped. The toes were wider, and the foot proportions were broader. When the length was compared to the width, the footprint formed a "U" shape. Herbivorous dinosaurs had more rounded tips on their toes.

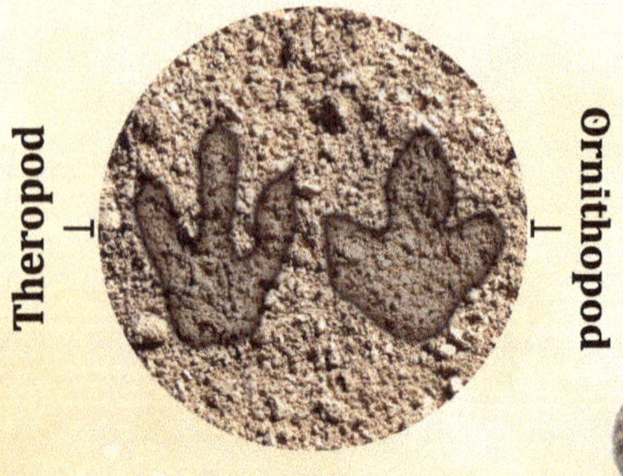

Theropod

Ornithopod

Theropod

Ornithopods were usually runners and grazers, herbivorous in nature. They were known as one of the most successful groups of herbivores during the Cretaceous period. Shantungosaurus was one of the longest known Ornithopods to have ever existed. It was also recognised as the largest known Ornithischian and the largest non-Sauropod dinosaur.

Barsboldia

Barsboldia was a large Ornithopod herbivore. It was a hadrosaurid dinosaur with a solid bone crest. Predatory threats primarily came from large predators such as Tyrannosaurus rex and Tarbosaurus. It measured up to 20 metres in length and was among the top ten longest-known dinosaurs.

Magnapaulia

The Magnapaulia was estimated to be about 41 feet long and was one among the longest known dinosaurs. Although they were not as large as Shantungosaurus, it was still vulnerable to attacks by large carnivores. It grazed on low-lying vegetation and had a distinctive duck-billed appearance.

Magnapaulia

Kritosaurus

The Kritosautus is a partially known duck-billed dinosaur that lived about 66 million years ago. They were one of the longest known hadrosaurids and weighed around 2.3 tonnes. They were herbivores who grazed on plants. The Kritosaurs were known for their flat heads and had a ridge of bone between their eyes. The front legs were rarely used for walking and may have been used for gathering food when required. They probably lived in herds and protected their young ones from large predators.

Huaxiaosaurus

Huaxiaosaurus was the largest and longest known hadrosaur. It measured 61 feet in length and weighed around 7 tonnes. It lived during the same period as Shantungosaurus, and its hind legs were exceptionally robust and muscular. It had long, heavy, muscular legs that provided balance and stability for its massive body. These dinosaurs represented the older and larger individuals of their species.

Kritosaurus

SAUROPOD DINOSAURS

Sauropod
Dinosaurs

The sauropods, meaning 'lizard-footed' in Greek, emerged during the Late Triassic period. They were known as the largest animals to have ever lived on land. By the Late Jurassic period, the sauropods existed in great numbers, especially the Diplodocid and Brachiosaurid species.

Largest Sauropods

The Seismosaurus, one of the longest dinosaurs, measured up to 45 metres in length. Brachiosaurids were extremely tall, possessing high shoulders and exceptionally long necks. Sauroposeidons were the tallest sauropods, reaching heights of 18 metres.

Size

The most defining characteristic of sauropods was their massive size, making them among the largest dinosaurs within the ecosystem. Some dwarf sauropods grew up to 5–6 metres in length. As the largest dinosaurs to have walked on land, sauropods shared similar physical features, with variations primarily in size. The only competitors to sauropods in terms of size within the entire animal kingdom were rorqual whales, such as modern-day blue whales.

Seismosaurus

Heaviest
Dinosaurs

With their enormous height and length, some of the heaviest sauropods included Argentinosauruses, which weighed around 100 metric tonnes. Other massive sauropods, such as Titanosaurs and Bruhathkayosauruses, weighed between 75 and 90 tonnes. Scientists believe these dinosaurs may have struggled to support their immense weight. By comparison, the largest land animal alive today, the African savannah elephant, weighs an average of 6 -7 tonnes.

Armours

The primary defence mechanism of sauropods against predators was their enormous size, which protected them from smaller carnivores. Their long tails were sometimes used as whips to deter attackers. Some sauropods developed additional protective features, such as body armour. Agustinias developed spines along their backs, while Shunosauruses had small, club-like structures on their tails. Saltasauruses and Ampelosauruses possessed bony plates emerging from their bodies for additional defence.

Egg Layers

As herbivorous creatures, sauropods shared common characteristics such as small heads, massive bodies, and long, counter-balancing tails. Many species were egg-laying dinosaurs, with evidence showing that Camarasauruses and Titanosaurs laid eggs. Sauropods had thick legs with blunt, narrow feet equipped with five toes to support their weight.

Argentinosaurus

Posture

Sauropods first evolved the ability to stand on their hind legs, using their tails for balance --a posture similar to a tripod stand. Research suggests that early sauropods initially stood on their hind legs to reach treetop vegetation. However, this stance placed immense stress on their tails.

Tail Fractures

As sauropods increased in size, the vertebrae near their tails bore an immense amount of weight. Since early sauropods stood on their hind legs, pressure on the tail may have led to spinal fractures. Over time, these dinosaurs likely returned to walking on all four legs. Scientists believe that the evolution of their tail spines served as a safety measure, preventing them from reverting to bipedal posture.

Sauropod Evolution

The first sauropods evolved around 200 million years ago, during the Mid-Jurassic period. The earliest true sauropods included Vulcanodon and Barapasaurus. Preceding sauropods were Prosauropods, which were significantly smaller. Among these, Anchisauruses and Massospondyluses were considered some of the earliest sauropodomorph dinosaurs.

Early Sauropods

In 2010, palaeontologists uncovered an entire sauropod skeleton, including its skull. One of the earliest true sauropods was Yizhousaurus, alongside another Asian sauropod, Isanosaurus, both of which lived around the Triassic-Jurassic boundary.

Jurassic Park Movie

The film Jurassic Park popularised the image of a sauropod standing on its hind legs. Brachiosaurus, the first fully shown dinosaur in the movie, did not actually rear up but used its long neck to reach high foliage while staying on all fours. Unlike plated dinosaurs like Stegosaurus, Brachiosaurus had no body armour, as it belonged to the sauropod group.

Vulcanodon

Sauropod
Lifestyle

The sauropods reached the peak of their dominance during the Late Jurassic period. Around 150 million years ago, fully grown adults dominated the land, as they could easily evade most predators. Although evidence suggests that a group of Allosauruses may have been capable of hunting an adult Diplodocus, other sauropods remained dominant herbivores. However, newborns and the aged and elderly sauropods would have been vulnerable prey for theropod dinosaurs.

Slow Extinction

During the Cretaceous period, sauropod populations gradually declined. By the time dinosaurs became extinct, only Titanosaurs remained, representing the last lineage of sauropods. By 65 million years ago, Titanosauruses and Rapetosauruses were the only known surviving sauropods.

Titanosaurs

Many Titanosaurs developed strong armour plating, which helped them adapt to climatic changes while providing protection against predators. The largest Titanosaurs, including Argentinosauruses, surpassed the size of even the biggest sauropods.

Titanosaurs

Sauropod Teeth

With respect to their size, sauropods were large eating machines. The adults gobbled down hundreds of pounds of plants and leaves every day in order to keep up their weight. Depending on their diets, sauropods had two kinds of teeth. One type was flat and spoon-shaped. These teeth were found in camarasaurs and brachiosaurs. Another type of teeth were thin and peglike as found in the Diplodocus.

Diplodocus Teeth

The Diplodocus had a unique skull structure and body design. It was believed to have had a weak bite force but a high tooth replacement rate, generating one new tooth approximately every 35 days. Diplodocuses were known for bark stripping and feeding on branches. They co-existed with Camarasauruses, but their diets were entirely different from each other. Diplodocus teeth were best suited for consuming soft leaves from trees and ferns that grew close to the ground. Their "peg-like" teeth pointed forward, and due to their rapid tooth wear, Diplodocuses were not capable of chewing like other sauropods.

Camarasaurus

111

Sauropod Fossils

It is said that sauropods, being among the largest dinosaurs, left behind some of the most incomplete skeletons. While smaller dinosaurs, such as Microraptors, have been found as nearly complete fossils, fully intact sauropod skeletons are rare. Some sauropod fossils have even been discovered without their skulls. A fossilised bone once classified as belonging to an old Cetiosaurus remained uncertain until additional remains were found. Uncertainty in fossil identification led to Brontosaurus being renamed Apatosaurus, but recent studies suggest it may be a distinct genus. Similarly, Brachiosauruses were once mistakenly believed to be whale ancestors, thought to wade in seas with their long necks above water for breathing. Such misconceptions highlight evolving paleontological insights.

Gigantism

Sauropod gigantism was made possible by a specific combination of evolutionary innovations at multiple levels, leading to a remarkable evolutionary breakthrough. The most significant adaptation was the Sauropod Bauplan, which featured an exceptionally long neck. These long-necked dinosaurs had a greater food intake than other herbivores, as they could conveniently reach treetops. Sauropods absorbed more energy from their environment than other herbivorous dinosaurs.

Sauropod Brains

It was once commonly believed that sauropods had a second brain located at the base of their tails. However, scientists now suggest that what was previously thought to be a brain was actually an enlargement or swelling in the spinal cord. This swelling, roughly the size of a small animal's brain, contained fatty tissues and nerves. It was believed to assist in controlling the movements of the hind legs and tail. Among the sauropods with relatively larger brains were Algoasauruses, Aragosauruses, and Asiatosauruses.

Agustinia

A distinctive feature observed in some sauropods was their tough body armour, such as the spiky knobs found on Agustinias. Unlike most terrestrial vertebrates, these dinosaurs had their nostrils positioned on their skulls rather than at the snout. They also possessed spiky osteoderms, which were thought to be fragments of their hips and ribs, providing them with additional protection.

Sauropod Diet

The sauropods usually consumed conifers, which were found in abundance during the period when sauropods existed. Other food sources included gingkos, seed ferns, cycads, horsetails and much more. The sauropods that lived in the mid-Cretaceous and Late Cretaceous periods ate flowering plants. Different sauropods atw different types of herbs and plants like the Brachiosaurs.

Algoasaurus

These sauropods were geographically widespread and were found living in South Africa. They were found living during the Late Jurassic period and went on to live till the Early Cretaceous period. Measuring about 9 metres in length, they were herbivores. They were often classified as Titanosaurids. Known as the 'Algoa Bay reptiles,' they were a group of neosauropods.

Aragosaurus

Aragosaurus eggs, like those of other sauropods, resembled present-day goose eggs. These dinosaurs, meaning "Aragon lizards," lived around 125 million years ago and were structurally similar to Camarasauruses. They had short, compact skulls and exceptionally long necks. Their large, broad teeth were well suited for slicing through the leaves and branches of tall conifer trees.

Asiatosaurus

The Asiatosauruses, meaning "Asian lizards," lived during the Early Cretaceous period. Their fossils have been discovered in China and Mongolia. They had Camarasaurus-like teeth and grew up to approximately 30 metres in length, weighing as much as 45 tonnes.

Egg Shells

The eggshells of sauropods were not as smooth as they appeared. If observed under a microscope, many small visible pores could be seen. These pores functioned as tiny canals that regulated moisture levels, allowing the developing dinosaur to breathe within the egg. The number, size, and shape of these pores differed from species to species. The structure of the eggshells provided insight into nesting behaviours, revealing where dinosaurs laid their eggs and how they built their nests. Highly porous eggs dried out quickly, whereas eggs with numerous large pores were likely kept in stable positions and well protected from predators.

Camarasaurus

Camarasauruses were not well adapted for an aquatic lifestyle. They had relatively small, weak tails, blunt heads, and spoon-shaped teeth. While some studies suggest that Camarasauruses were efficient waders, others indicate that they lacked any significant adaptations for swimming.

Camarasaurus

115

Jurassic
Sauropods

Although sauropods evolved during the Cretaceous period, they were dominant during the Jurassic period. In both North America and Europe, the Jurassic period marked the peak of their reign. By around 145 million years ago, during the Cretaceous period, the number of sauropods began to decline. However, much later, other sauropods re-emerged, re-establishing their presence in Europe and North America.

Barosaurus

Barosauruses were large, long-necked herbivores that thrived during the Late Jurassic period, around 156 million years ago. Their name, meaning 'heavy lizards,' reflected their enormous size. They were slow-moving creatures, growing up to 80 feet in length and weighing between 12 and 20 tonnes. Their primary defence against predators was their sheer size.

Janenschia

Janenschias lived during the Jurassic period, approximately 150 million years ago. They may have been covered in armoured plates, though no fossil evidence confirms this. They had long necks and tails, weighed around 33 tonnes, and measured about 80 feet in length. Like other sauropods, Janenschias hatched from eggs, and it is presumed that they laid their eggs while walking. Among sauropods, Janenschias were thought to have had the lowest intelligence.

Barosaurus

Growth and Development

Mamenchisaurus

Mamenchisauruses were large sauropods whose fossils were discovered in China. These dinosaurs lived around 160 million years ago and laid approximately 25 to 30 eggs at a time. They weighed around 13 tonnes and consumed nearly 1,150 pounds of food per day. They had 30-foot-long necks and small skulls. It is believed that Mamenchisauruses moved in large herds. On average, an adult Mamenchisaurus reached about 60 feet in length.

Sauropod Growth

Compared to human babies, which double in weight in approximately five months, sauropod hatchlings doubled in weight in just five days. Adolescent sauropods gained roughly 3,500 pounds per year. Their growth rate surpassed that of the heaviest modern reptiles. Sauropods reached full size by their third decade of life. Their hearts beat fewer than 10 times per minute, compared to an average human heart rate of 72 beats per minute.

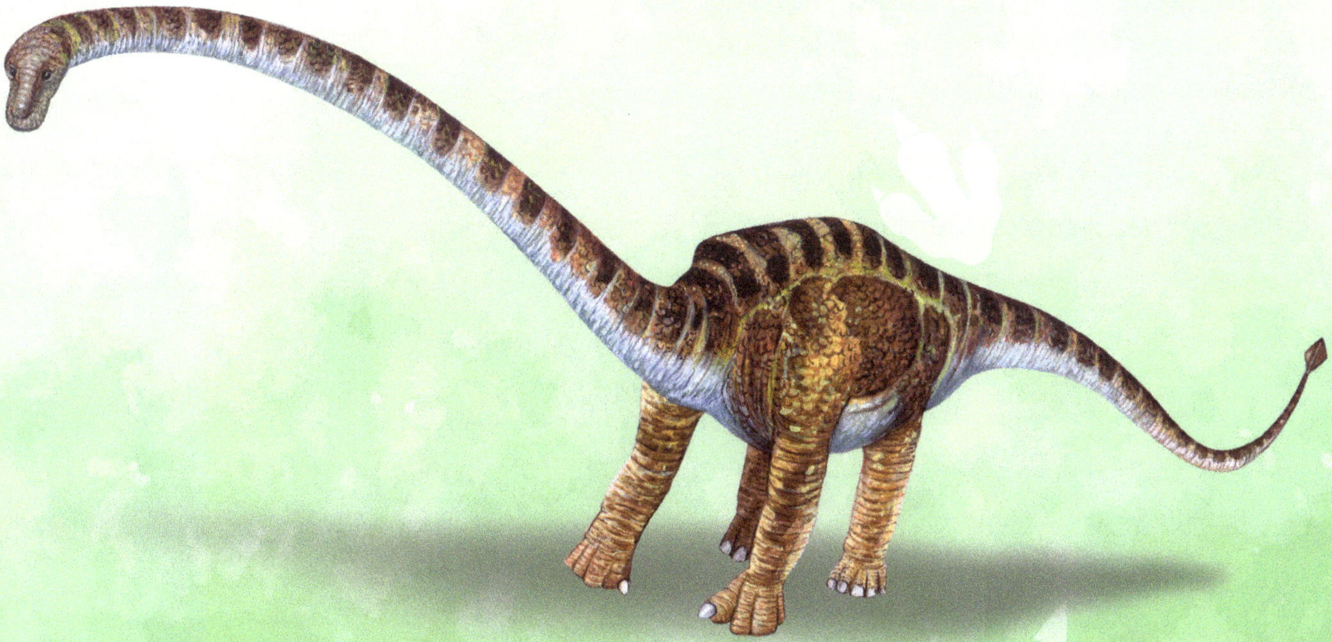

Mamenchisaurus

Sauropod Dinosaurs

Diplodocus

Diplodocuses are among the most well-known sauropods. They are famous for being among the longest dinosaurs to have ever walked the Earth. A group of closely related dinosaurs within the genus Diplodocidae shared similar characteristics to Diplodocus. Diplodocuses remained stationary while sweeping their long necks across large trees to feed. on large trees for food. This allowed them to coexist with other sauropods. Especially they lived alongside Brachiosauruses.

Amphicoelias

A significant discovery made in North America during the "Bone Wars" led scientists to believe that Amphicoeliases were among the largest dinosaurs, second only to Argentinosauruses. However, due to the rarity of their fossils, making precise estimates about their lifestyle and exact size has been challenging.

Brachiosaurus

Brachiosaurus

Sauropods are typically recognised for their long necks, but Brachiosauruses had comparatively shorter necks yet were among the tallest sauropods. They belonged to the clade Macronaria and were capable of reaching treetops at greater heights than many other herbivorous dinosaurs, including Stegosauruses, Ornithopods, and other sauropods.

Rapetosaurus

The Rapetosauruses were among the most famous Titanosaurs, as they were the only dinosaurs whose complete skeletons were discovered in fossil research. These sauropods were initially around eight metres long as juveniles, but they could grow up to fifteen metres in length. Due to the abundance of information obtained from their complete fossils, Rapetosauruses have been widely used as reference specimens for identifying other Titanosaur species.

Saltasaurus

Saltasauruses were not as large as many other sauropods, but they had a unique distinguishing feature. They possessed armour plating beneath their skin, consisting of rough, bony scales. This natural defence mechanism provided protection against predators such as Carcharodontosauruses, which were known for tearing flesh from the body of their prey during attacks.

Saltasaurus

Supersaurus

Supersauruses, meaning "super lizards," were Diplodocid dinosaurs that were first discovered in the Late Jurassic period. These herbivorous dinosaurs had unique features such as long necks and whip-like tails. Their (sauropods) respiratory systems included air sacs in the neck, allowing their lungs to rest while the air sacs facilitated respiration. These dinosaurs lived between 142 and 154 million years ago.

Sauroposeidon

Sauroposeidons were discovered in what are now the states of Oklahoma and Texas and lived during the Early Cretaceous period. They were the last great sauropods to be found in North America before all sauropods became extinct. As Brachiosaurid dinosaurs, their heads could reach heights of up to 18 metres, making them among the tallest known dinosaurs.

Antarctica Fossil

The first sauropod fossils discovered in Antarctica were estimated to be between 70 and 80 million years old. Although the remains were too incomplete to be given a definitive name, they were unique enough to be identified as belonging to a Titanosaur. This discovery marked the first recorded evidence of sauropods in Antarctica.

SEA DINOSAURS

Sea Dinosaurs

The largest dinosaurs were the most ferocious dinosaurs that ever walked the earth, on land. Dating back to 200 million years ago, sea monsters ruled the seas. There were dinosaurs, reptiles and fishes that were heavier than the present day blue whales.

Dakosaurus

Dakosauruses lived in Germany and had unusual reptilian bodies but resembled fish. They were among the top marine predators during the Jurassic period. Often compared to modern crocodiles, they could grow up to 16 feet in length. Fossils of Dakosauruses have been found in the seas of England, Russia, and Argentina.

Shastasaurus

The Shastasaurus is the largest marine predator ever found. They looked like modern dolphins and could grow up to 65 feet in length. Even though they were the largest predators to rule the seas, they were not ferocious or dangerous. They fed on small fish and lived during the Triassic period.

Shastasaurus

Top Predators

The top predators of the seas during the dinosaur period were sea monsters. They co-existed with terrestrial dinosaurs and ruled the seas. They resembled modern day reptiles and fishes and fed on smaller sea animals including planktons.

Mosasaurus

The Mosasaurus is an extinct group of large marine predators that lived during the Late Cretaceous period. They were aquatic lizards and one of the largest predators of the sea. Their jaws were lined with massive teeth and they had paddle-like limbs. They had large tails that resembled upside down modern-day sharks tails.

Thalassomedon

They were a genus of plesiosaur meaning 'sea lords'. The Thalassomedons were massive predators and reached lengths up to 35 feet. They were equipped with unique flippers which reached 5 metres in length and helped them paddle across water. They were known as the top predators throughout the Cretaceous period.

Mosasaurus

Tylosaurus

Tylosauruses belonged to the Mosasaur family and could grow to nearly 50 feet in length. As carnivorous predators, they had a diverse diet, feeding on sharks, fish, plesiosaurs, other mosasaurs, and even some birds. They were among the top predators of the Late Cretaceous period and remained at the top of the food chain for millions of years.

Tanystropheus

Tanystropheuses were not strictly marine reptiles, but their diet consisted primarily of fish. They could also live on land, though scientists believe they spent most of their time in the sea. These reptiles had extremely long necks and reached lengths of up to 20 feet. They lived during the Early Triassic period, nearly 215 million years ago.

Nothosaurs

The Nothosaurs grew up to 13 feet in length and were very aggressive hunters. They had a mouth full of massive teeth that were sharp and outward-pointing. They preyed on squid and small fish. They had a reptilian look and attacked their prey by sneaking up on them and taking them down by surprise. The Nothosaurs were deep-sea predators and lived 200 million years ago.

Tylosaurus

Megalodon

Regarded as some of the largest and most fearsome predators in marine history, Megalodons were terrifying prehistoric sharks. They were much larger and more powerful versions of today's great white sharks. Megalodons could grow up to 65 feet in length—longer than a school bus.

Liopleurodon

Liopleurodons were marine reptiles that grew to nearly 20 feet in length. They primarily inhabited the seas of Europe during the Jurassic period and were some of the most formidable sea predators. Their jaws, measuring a massive 10 feet in length, were lined with sharp teeth capable of easily tearing apart flesh.

Thalattoarchon

Thalattoarchons were the size of school buses, reaching lengths of up to 30 feet. They were a type of ichthyosaur that lived 244 million years ago during the Triassic period. Remarkably, they survived the mass extinction event that wiped out nearly 95% of marine life.

Megalodon

Ichthyosaurs

The Ichthyosaurs meaning 'fish lizard' were large marine reptiles that thrived during the Mesozoic era. They evolved into a group of sea reptiles first appeared in the Early Triassic period. The Ichthyosaur species grew from 1 metre to 16 metres long and had groups of sea reptiles that resembled modern day dolphins and whales.

Grippia

Grippias were a genus of ichthyosaurs that resembled modern dolphins. These small ichthyosaurs measured up to 1.5 metres in length. They preyed on armoured fish, including shellfish, and ate a variety of other fish. Scientists believe they were carnivorous reptiles that lived during the Triassic period.

Mixosaurus

Mixosauruses were mid-Triassic ichthyosaurs that grew up to 2 metres in length. Due to their long tails and relatively small fins, they were believed to be slow swimmers. They had narrow jaws lined with numerous sharp teeth, ideal for catching fish. The name Mixosaurus, meaning "mixed lizard," signifies their transitional form between eel-shaped and dolphin-shaped marine reptiles.

Ichthyosaurus

Shonisaurus

The Shonisaurus was a genus of ichthyosaur that lived during the Late Triassic period. They were marine adapted reptiles and lived across oceans worldwide. They had unusual appearances, resembling dolphins but growing significantly larger. They could reach up to 50 feet in length and weigh around 30 tonnes, primarily feeding on fish and squid. One fascinating feature of Shonisauruses was that while they were born with teeth, they lost them as they matured.

Himalayasaurus

Himalayasauruses were an extinct group of ichthyosaurs discovered in Tibet. Their entire bodies measured up to 15 metres in length. They were given this name due to the lack of defining features that categorised them as typical ichthyosaurs. These large-bodied marine reptiles, similar to Shastasauruses, lived during the Late Triassic period.

Californosaurus

Californosauruses were extinct marine reptiles found in what is now California. They were among the earliest advanced forms of ichthyosaurs. With long, eel-like tails, they were capable of fast swimming. Their teeth and jawlines provided evidence that they hunted faster-swimming fish. Californosauruses had wide fins that helped them paddle swiftly across the water.

Shonisaurus

Prehistoric
Sea Monsters

Although the seas of today's world behold scary sea monsters such as the piranhas, blue whales, great white sharks and more, they are nothing compared to the sea monsters of the dinosaur period. With giant sea lizards and monster sharks that roamed the oceans, they were equivalent to the T.Rex and other land predators.

Helicoprion

These prehistoric sharks grew up to 15 feet in length and had a unique lower jaw featuring a "tooth whorl." Helicoprions were definite carnivores, and their teeth resembled a circular saw. They primarily fed on softer prey such as jellyfish. They survived the mass extinction at the end of the Triassic period and lived in the deep seas.

Basilosaurus

Basilosauruses were not reptiles but early whales. They were ancestors of modern whales and grew up to 85 feet long. They were described as "snake-whales" due to their elongated bodies. Unlike modern whales, they lacked echolocation and advanced cognitive abilities, instead swimming across the oceans, feeding on smaller fish and plankton.

Basilosaurus

Giant Stingray

The Giant Stingray grows up to 17 feet in length and has a 10-inch-long poisonous tails. They existed from the dinosaur ages and survived all kinds of ice ages and extinctions. Stingrays continued to thrive even after the dinosaurs went extinct, making them one of the most successful marine species.

Livyatan Melvillei

The Livyatan was a hypercarnivorous whale that ate other whales. They were the largest predators of the sea with massive teeth that grew up to 1.18 feet. They probably co-existed and grew in the same seas as the Megaladon and had to compete with other large predators of the sea.

Kronosaurus

The Kronosaurs were short-necked pliosaurs and grew up to 30 feet long. They had a massive mouth that was lined with teeth measuring 11 inches long. They were named Kronosaurs, after 'kronus', the king of the Greek Titans, due to their massive size and predatory dominance.

Livyatan Melvillei

Cretaceous
Sea Giants

The Cretaceous marine life consisted of scary sea giants that dominated the era. Kansas was famous for coming up with marine reptile fossils of fish that thrived during the Cretaceous period. The Kansas sea bed was home to large sea giants that lived 75 million years ago.

Elasmosaurus

Elasmosauruses were some of the most remarkable sea monsters that lived 85 million years ago. They had extremely long necks and small heads, which deceived their prey into thinking they were much smaller predators. This advantage allowed them to ambush fish, as their large bodies remained hidden behind them. Uniquely, they supplemented their diet by swallowing stones.

Halisaurus

Closely related to snakes, Halisauruses were monstrous open-water predators. They had extremely long tails, making up more than half of their body length, and could grow up to 13 feet long. Living 86 million years ago, they swallowed their prey whole, feeding on small fish, molluscs, and sea birds.

Elasmosaurus

Killer Fish

Commonly called "Killer Fish," Xiphactinuses grew up to 20 feet in length. They were vigorous hunters, actively chasing large fish across the seas. They were incredibly fast swimmers and could leap out of the water like modern dolphins. Their jaws were designed to open exceptionally wide to accommodate large prey. Their hunting speed was unmatched by any other marine predator of their time.

Largest Turtle

Archelons were the largest turtles to have ever swum in the Cretaceous oceans. They spent most of their time feeding on jellyfish and ammonites, only coming onto land to lay eggs, much like modern turtles. Occasionally, they grazed on seaweed and spent long periods resting on the seabed. They weighed up to 2 tonnes and had wide, paddle-like limbs that allowed them to move slowly through the water. Archelons lived for millions of years and had an exceptionally long lifespan.

Xiphactinus

Long-Necked
Beasts

During the Late Triassic period, about 205 million years ago, a new species of marine reptiles emerged They had magnificently long necks and were uniquely structured. Scientists named them 'Plesiosaurs'. Their unusual long necks made it appear like they were snakes with a large body attached.

Plesiosaurs

The first fossil of a Plesiosaur was an Elasmosaurus. Plesiosauruses had extremely small and delicate skulls, often no larger than the diameter of their long necks. These creatures were 42 feet long, with nearly 23 feet of their body made up of their necks. They had an astonishing 72 vertebrae in their necks, compared to present-day giraffes, which have only seven.

Pliosaurs

The Pliosaurs fall under the same category as long-necked dinosaurs. They co-existed with the Plesiosaurs and scientists believe that these creatures were pure meat eaters. Their diet included molluscs, fish and squid. They had broad, streamlined bodies.

Plesiosaurs

Many sea monsters were either reptiles or resembled modern sharks, dolphins, crocodiles and turtles. There were a few strange inhabitants of the sea who stood apart from all other marine creatures.

Stethacanthus

Stethacanthuses resembled modern-day sharks except for their unusual dorsal fins, which were shaped like ironing boards. The tops of these fins were covered in tooth-shaped scales, similar to the patch of skin on their snouts. Stethacanthuses were migratory creatures, moving to different locations to mate and give birth.

Odobenocetops

Odobenocetopses were strange-looking creatures that resembled a cross between walruses and manatees. They lacked teeth and fed on small worms and shellfish. They thrived in shallow waters and seabeds, where they found the safest environments to live. Odobenocetopses were air-breathing marine animals, surfacing periodically to take in oxygen. Their muscular lips allowed them to extract shellfish from their shells.

Odobenocetops

133

Leedsichthys

Leedsichthyses were gentle giant fish that dwarfed every other marine fish during the dinosaur era. They were not massive predators but fed on small animals and shellfish. They swam slowly through the upper ocean waters, taking mouthfuls of plankton-rich water. They dominated the Jurassic seas but had no defence mechanisms other than their massive size. Though undefeated by most predators, minor wounds from attacks could lead to a slow decline as they aged.

Sea Scorpions

Sea scorpions were the largest arthropods to have ever lived during the dinosaur era. Their pincers grew significantly larger in later evolutionary stages. They primarily inhabited freshwater environments and occasionally ventured onto land. They were closely related to crabs, horseshoe crabs, spiders, and scorpions. Poisonous by nature, they survived into the Permian period.

Leedsichthys

Cymbospondylus

Cymbospondyluses were members of the ichthyosaur family. They were powerful, dolphin-like swimmers with sharp teeth. These apex predators ruled the Triassic seas and had no dorsal fins, instead possessing eel-shaped tails. Their skulls measured around 1 metre in length and were equipped with short, sharp teeth perfect for catching fish and large reptiles. Unlike many reptiles, Cymbospondyluses gave birth to live young rather than laying eggs.

Metriorhynchus

Metriorhynchuses were shorter than any modern-day crocodiles, measuring around 3 metres in length. However, they were far deadlier than any living sea creature. These marine crocodiles hunted pterosaurs mid-flight. They were powerful predators, taking down their prey with a single powerful strike from their muscular tails.

Giant Orthocone

Giant orthocones were formidable predators that lived 450 million years ago. Shaped like jet-propelled cones, they used tentacles for locomotion. Growing up to 11 metres in length, they moved through the water by expelling water in the opposite direction. Both their mouths and tentacles emerged from one end of their shells. They seized their prey using tentacles and tore their flesh apart with beak-like mouths.

Giant Orthocone

Styxosaurus

Styxosauruses belonged to the family of plesiosaurs and lived during the Cretaceous period, around 85 million years ago. They grew up to 11 metres in length and had sharp, pointed teeth ideal for seizing and gripping prey. Their long necks allowed them to sneak up on schools of fish and swallow them whole. Their flipper-like paddles enabled them to move efficiently through the water.

Platecarpus

Platecarpuses, meaning "flat wrist," were an extinct group of aquatic lizards belonging to the mosasaur family in the Late Cretaceous period. They had downturned tails and steering flippers. Their skulls were shorter, and they had fewer teeth compared to other mosasaurs. They grew up to 4 metres in length and possessed eel-like tails, which functioned as strong swimming aids, improving their speed.These prehistoric creatures existed throughout the dinosaur era. Just as Tyrannosauruses rex and other massive allosauruses ruled the land, kings and rulers of the seas reigned beneath the waves.

Styxosaurus

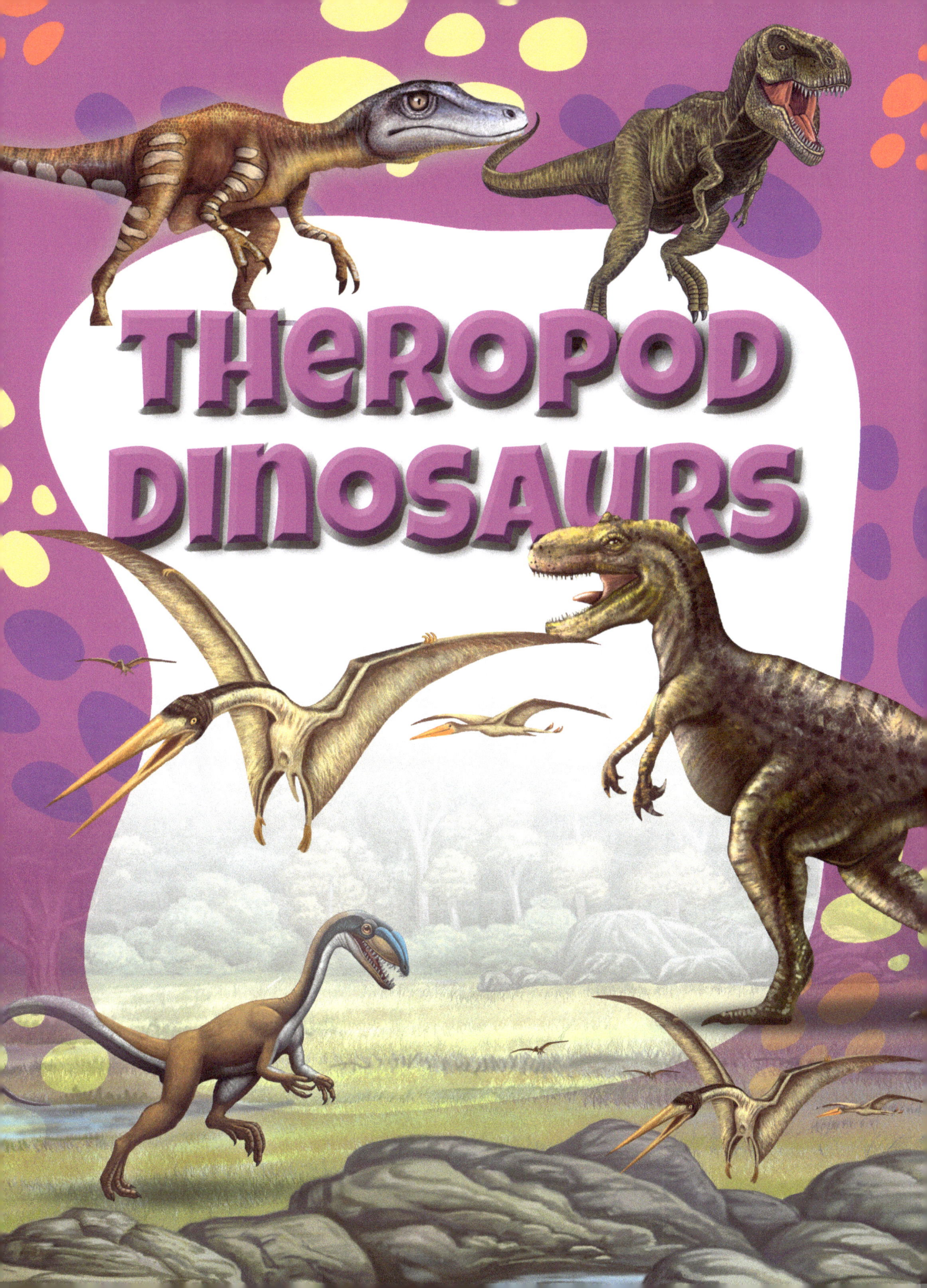

THEROPOD DINOSAURS

Theropod Dinosaurs

Theropods, meaning "beast-footed" dinosaurs, belong to the suborder of the Saurischian dinosaurs. These dinosaurs first appeared in the late Triassic Period. The famous theropod dinosaurs include the Allosaurus, the Spinosaurus and the Tyrannosaurus Rex.

Tyrannosaurus Rex

Tyrannosauruses rex were among the largest meat-eating dinosaurs that ever walked the Earth. With 4-foot jaws designed for maximum bone-crushing action, they were called the "Kings of Predators." These Theropods were famous for their monstrous structures and tiny forelimbs that resembled hands with nearly opposable thumbs. They measured up to 40 feet in length and about 20 feet in height, with massive 5-foot-long skulls. They could consume up to 500 pounds of flesh in a single meal.

Allosaurus

Allosauruses were among the earliest dinosaurs discovered, with fossils found in abundance. These dinosaurs lived 155 million years ago, during the Late Jurassic period. Their name, meaning "Different Lizard," reflected their unique characteristics. They grew up to 43 feet in length and 16 feet in height. As massive carnivores, Allosauruses weighed approximately 1,500 kilograms. With their short necks and narrow, elongated skulls, they were capable of killing and feasting on healthy herbivores and sauropods.

Allosaurus

Spinosaurus

Spinosauruses, known for their seven-foot-long spines, lived 100 million years ago during the Cretaceous period. They were well adapted for aquatic life, possessing crocodile-like teeth capable of tearing into large fish. Known as the world's largest meat-eating dinosaurs, the sail-backed "Spine Lizards" weighed up to 20 tonnes and measured up to 60 feet in length.

Therizinosaurus

These Theropods were unique as they were solely herbivorous. They had giant, razor-sharp claws that may have been used for digging, grasping, and piercing. Changes in their claw structures suggest that they may have evolved into birds in later generations. Therizinosaurs lived during the Late Cretaceous period. They were estimated to weigh five tonnes and reach 33 feet in height. Their forelimbs measured up to 8 feet in length, and their claws were the largest known among all dinosaurs.

Velociraptor

Velociraptors, meaning "Speedy Thieves," had sharp claws measuring up to 3.5 inches on each limb. These carnivores hunted smaller herbivores and other predators. They always moved in herds. Velociraptors lived about 75 million years ago, during the Late Cretaceous period.

Spinosaurus

Giganotosaurus

Giganotosauruses, among the largest Theropods, were known to grow even larger than Tyrannosauruses rex and hunted the massive Argentinosauruses. Descendants of Allosauruses, they lived alongside sauropods. These Theropods were considered the second-largest carnivorous dinosaurs, with massive skulls and long tails that helped maintain balance. They had three-clawed fingers and muscular limbs that enabled them to run at speeds of up to 51 km/h. With over 60 blade-like teeth measuring 8 inches in length, Giganotosauruses were among the most feared dinosaurs, capable of easily tearing flesh and crushing bones.

Carcharodontosaurus

Carcharodontosauruses existed between 112 and 93 million years ago, during the mid-Cretaceous period. They were among the largest Theropods, growing even larger than Giganotosauruses. These formidable predators weighed around 15 tonnes and grew up to 44 feet in length. Measuring 13 feet high at the hips, they were some of the fiercest competitors among Theropods.

Giganotosaurus

Theropod Diet

All early Theropods were primarily carnivorous. Fossils have revealed sharp, flesh-tearing teeth and clear predatory behaviours. A Compsognathus fossil was found with a lizard in its stomach, confirming its diet. However, Therizinosaurs had large abdomens for digesting plant matter and small, leaf-shaped teeth for cutting through vegetation. Some Maniraptors exhibited adaptations for omnivorous diets.

Hyper Carnivores

Some Theropods, such as Tyrannosauruses rex and Velociraptors, were classified as "hyper-carnivores," meaning they were primarily meat-eaters but occasionally consumed plant matter. A famous fossil shows a Velociraptor locked in combat with a Protoceratops. A recent study found that out of 90 Theropod species, 44 were found to have a predominantly plant-based diet. Herbivorous Theropods, such as Therizinosaurs, are examples of vegetarian dinosaurs.

Maniraptors

Many species of Maniraptors consumed plants as part of their diet. They are believed to have been the common ancestors of all hyper-carnivores. Predatory Maniraptors, such as Velociraptors, are thought to have re-evolved from vegetarian ancestors.

Therizinosaurs

Largest Theropods

Saurophaganax

Saurophaganaxes, meaning "Lizard-Eating Masters," lived approximately 150 million years ago, during the Late Jurassic period. These dinosaurs measured around 43 feet in length and 14 feet in height, weighing between 3 and 4 tonnes. Due to their large size, food availability was a challenge, leading them to scavenge or steal meals from other dinosaurs.

Tyrannotitan

Tyrannotitans were Theropod dinosaurs that lived 120 million years ago, in the Early Cretaceous period. These dinosaurs measured up to 15 metres in length and 7 metres in height. Large Theropods found in Argentina, they had tiny forearms and thick skulls. Tyrannotitans, meaning "Tyrant Titans," weighed up to 7 tonnes and could reach speeds of up to 20 miles per hour.

Mapusaurus

Measuring up to 40 feet in length and weighing 4 tonnes, Mapusauruses, meaning "Earth Lizards," were massive Theropods that lived 100 million years ago. Unlike many other large carnivores, they travelled in packs and hunted in coordinated groups.

Tyrannotitan

Megalosaurus

Megalosauruses were large meat-eating dinosaurs that lived approximately 180 million years ago. They were the first dinosaurs to have their fossils formally described. Megalosauruses grew up to 30 feet in length and 10 feet in height. These large carnivores hunted even the enormous sauropods. Weighing around 1 tonne, Megalosauruses were also believed to have scavenged for food when necessary.

Megaraptor

Megaraptors were large, bird-like, terrifying meat-eaters with two enormous toe claws. With curved, flexible necks and large heads, Megaraptors were carnivores equipped with sharp teeth. If they hunted in packs, it is believed that they could take down any predator they desired. They had serrated teeth and powerful jaws capable of tearing apart any type of flesh.

Ornithomimus

Ornithomimuses were about 20 feet long and 8 feet tall, resembling ostriches. These Theropods were omnivores, feeding on both plants and small reptiles. Walking on two long, slender legs, Ornithomimuses lived during the Late Jurassic period, approximately 75 million years ago. They had long tails, long necks, and clawed fingers on each hand.

Ornithomimus

143

Evolution of Birds

Feathered Theropods

Evidence suggests that birds are a group of Theropods that survived beyond the mass extinction of the Late Cretaceous period. Around 9,000 bird species evolved from dinosaurs. Scientists believe that birds and dinosaurs share over 100 similarities, much like how humans and other mammals are related.

Archaeopteryx

Archaeopteryxes shared unique features with small carnivorous Theropods. With nearly 84 similarities to birds, Archaeopteryxes are considered the ancestors of modern birds. They were non-avian, feathered dinosaurs that possibly evolved into present-day bird species. Many of their bones were reduced and fused, increasing their flight efficiency.

Compsognathus

Small Theropods like Compsognathuses were among the first dinosaurs to develop feathers. They had short, hair-like feathers on their small heads, necks, and bodies. These feathers likely provided insulation. The different colour combinations of these feathers are believed to have contributed to the evolution of modern birds.

Archaeopteryx

Coelurosaur

The Coelurosaur is a sub-group of the theropods which is closely related to birds. Most of the feathered dinosaurs have been found under this classification. The Coelurosaur, meaning 'hollow-tailed lizard', had long arms and hinge-like ankles. The major groups of Coelurosaur include Albertosaurus, Gallimimus and Troodontids.

Albertosaurus

Albertosauruses lived around 70 million years ago, coexisting with Tyrannosauruses rex during the Late Cretaceous period. Fully grown Albertosauruses measured up to 40 feet in length and weighed around 8 tonnes. They were less than half the size of Tyrannosauruses rex but were fearsome killing machines that preyed on smaller Theropods and duck-billed dinosaurs.

Gallimimus

Gallimimuses resembled large ostriches with long tails and claws. These dinosaurs were among the fastest land carnivores. They had small, toothless beaks, long necks, and short arms. Living around 70 million years ago, they weighed approximately 990 pounds. Gallimimuses, meaning "Chicken Mimics," fed on plants, seeds, small reptiles, and fruits.

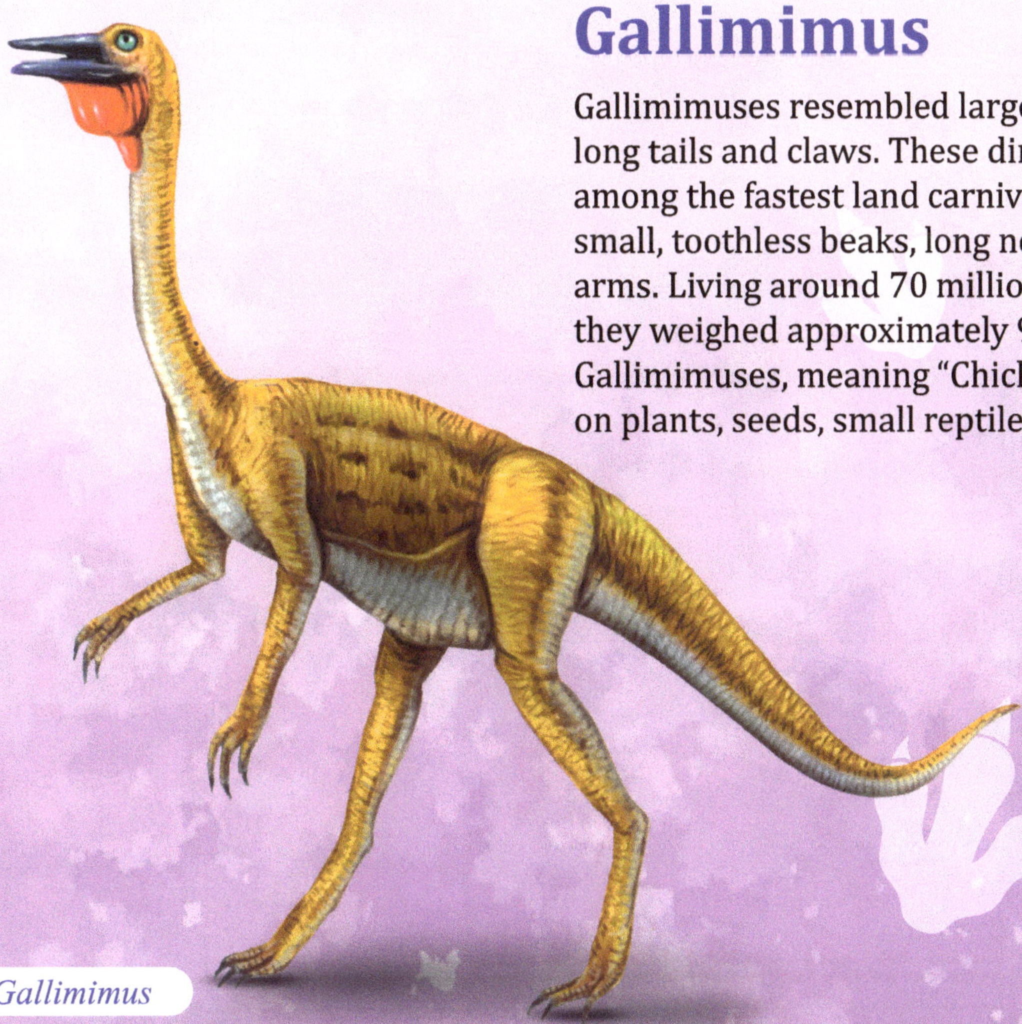

Gallimimus

Baby Louie

A new bird-like dinosaur fossil was discovered in China in 1993 but was initially ignored. After 25 years, the fossil was re-examined and determined to belong to the Late Cretaceous period, around 90 million years ago. Baby Louie's mother was an Oviraptorosaur, a winged species that would have grown to the size of an elephant.

Theropod Horns

Some Theropods, including Tyrannosauruses rex and Albertosauruses, had small, horn-like protrusions on their skulls. Scientists believe that these horns were used to signal other Theropods and served as a mode of communication and intimidation. These structures played a role in their evolutionary development.

Troodontids

Though Troodontids, meaning "Isolated Teeth," had bird-like features, they were unable to lift their feet high off the ground. Growing up to 3 metres in length, they were smaller compared to other Theropods. These dinosaurs were considered some of the most intelligent species based on their brain size. Troodontids were turkey-sized, had sickle claws, and possessed raptor-like hands. The largest Troodontid was Troodon, meaning "Wounding Tooth."

Troodontids

Brazilian Dinosaurs

Guaibasaurus

Guaibasauruses, meaning "Guaíba Lizards," were basal dinosaurs that lived during the Late Triassic period. These Theropods had three full fingers and two vestigial ones on each hand. As one of the earliest dinosaurs, Guaibasauruses did not share many characteristics with later dinosaurs. Although their fossils have not been fully discovered, some information about them is known. Unlike most Theropods, Guaibasauruses were herbivores that lived around 220 million years ago.

Ceratosauria

Ceratosaurias were among the earliest Theropods, dating back approximately 225 million years. The largest Ceratosaurias measured up to 25 feet in length and had prominent nasal horns. These Theropods had hollow bones and exhibited "bird-like" characteristics in later evolutionary stages. Fossils of Ceratosaurias have been found from around 145 million years ago, in the Late Jurassic period.

Tetanurae

Typical features of large Theropods in the Tetanurae group included enlarged hands, less flexible tails, and a reduction in the number of fingers compared to other Theropods. Tetanurae ranged from small bird-like dinosaurs that fed on seeds and plants to large packs of carnivores that hunted powerful predators. This Theropod group existed during the Cretaceous period and included early birds as part of their evolutionary lineage.

Ceratosauria

Theropod Swimmers

Sinocalliopteryx

Sinocalliopteryxes, meaning "Chinese Beautiful Feather," were small prehistoric Theropods that measured about 2 metres in length and stood 1.8 metres tall. These dinosaurs preyed on smaller lizards. Their claws were feathered, and evidence suggests that Sinocalliopteryxes were excellent swimmers. Fossilised river-bottom claw marks in China provide further proof that dinosaurs swam across seas, with Sinocalliopteryxes being among them.

Megapnosaurus

Megapnosauruses were occasional swimmers and crossed rivers and lakes when necessary. Megapnosauruses, meaning "Big Dead Lizards," were six-foot-long, meat-eating dinosaurs that lived 180 million years ago, during the Early Jurassic period. Packs of these dinosaurs were believed to have been wiped out in a flash flood while hunting. They were nocturnal hunters and were thought to have swum in rivers in search of food. Their lifespan was around seven years. Megapnosauruses were also referred to as "Syntaruses."

Megapnosaurus

Pterosaur

Birds are said to have developed flight adaptations similar to those of Pterosaurs. These adaptations include pneumatic bones, feathers, wings, and small teeth embedded in jaw sockets. Pterosaurs lived 150 million years ago and had legs shaped like those of modern birds. Their bird-like lungs allowed them to fly long distances efficiently.

Hollow Bones

Elongated legs and clawed hands provided strong support for the evolutionary link between birds and dinosaurs. The hollow, thin-walled bones of Archaeopteryxes provide strong evidence that birds evolved from Theropods, which share this feature. Many Theropods had curved necks and three-fingered limbs, further proving their ancestral relationship with birds. Ceratosaurians exhibited air-filled spaces in their bones, a trait associated with birds.

Scales and Feathers

It is believed that feathered Theropods first evolved during the Mesozoic era. Birds were identified as close relatives of dinosaurs after the discovery of prominent avian features in Archaeopteryxes. Scientists believe that bird evolution began with small raptors like Microraptors and Anchiornises, which had long, feathered legs that may have later evolved into wings.

Pterosaur

Dwarf Sauropod

In comparison to the smallest Theropods, the Titanosaur Magyarosauruses were around 6 metres long and weighed approximately 1 tonne. They had a strange, armoured body covering. Compared to other Titanosaurs, Magyarosauruses were relatively small and were named "Dwarf Titanosaurs." They are often referred to as the "smallest of the largest" dinosaurs within the Sauropod group.

Saurischians

Saurischians were divided into two groups: the fearsome, meat-eating Theropods and the calm, plant-eating Sauropods. Theropods walked on large hind legs, and their small front limbs were equipped with claws for grasping prey. In contrast, Sauropods had long necks that allowed them to reach treetops to graze on foliage. Sauropods, meaning "Lizard Feet," walked on all four legs.

Smallest Theropod

Although Theropods are typically associated with large sizes, some of the smallest Theropods, such as Compsognathuses, lived during the Triassic period. These human-sized dinosaurs coexisted with Sauropods and weighed around 3 kg. Compsognathuses are considered some of the smallest dinosaurs ever known, measuring approximately 1 metre in length.

Compsognathus

Basal Theropods

Eoraptor

Known as one of the earliest known dinosaurs, this basal Theropod lived around 230 million years ago. Eoraptors, meaning "Dawn Plunderers," were named due to their existence at the dawn of the dinosaur period. They had unusually long necks compared to other reptiles of their time. These dinosaurs used their small hind limbs to chase down smaller predators.

Herrerasaurus

Classified among the "Earliest Dinosaurs," Herrerasauruses, meaning "Herrera's Lizards," lived around 231 million years ago. These dinosaurs had sliding lower jaws that allowed them to prey on smaller reptiles efficiently. Initially classified as Sauropods, they were later recognised as basal Theropods, meaning "meat-eating dinosaurs."

Staurikosaurus

These dinosaurs lived in Brazil during the Late Triassic period. Staurikosauruses, meaning "Lizards of the Southern Cross," were small dinosaurs that existed around 225 million years ago. Since it was difficult to find dinosaur fossils in the Southern Hemisphere, they were named after the star constellation The Southern Cross. Their long and thin tails helped them maintain balance while moving.

Smallest Theropods

Anchiornis

Anchiornises were among the smallest Theropods and were incapable of flight. Weighing only about 110 grams and measuring up to 1 foot in length, these dinosaurs formed an evolutionary link between dinosaurs and modern birds. Due to their small hind legs, they were not well adapted to fast running.

Parvicursor

Parvicursors, meaning "Small Runners," were the smallest known Theropods. Measuring only about 39 cm from head to tail, they are one of the smallest non-avian dinosaurs ever discovered. Parvicursors had long, slender legs adapted for running. Their small, stubby forelimbs were equipped with claws that were used for digging into the ground in search of food.

Bee Hummingbird

Bee Hummingbirds measured only 5 cm in length and are considered the smallest known dinosaurs among the Mesozoic Theropods. Their beaks measured up to 1.5 inches. These species evolved into modern birds and still exist today as the smallest birds on Earth.

Anchiornis

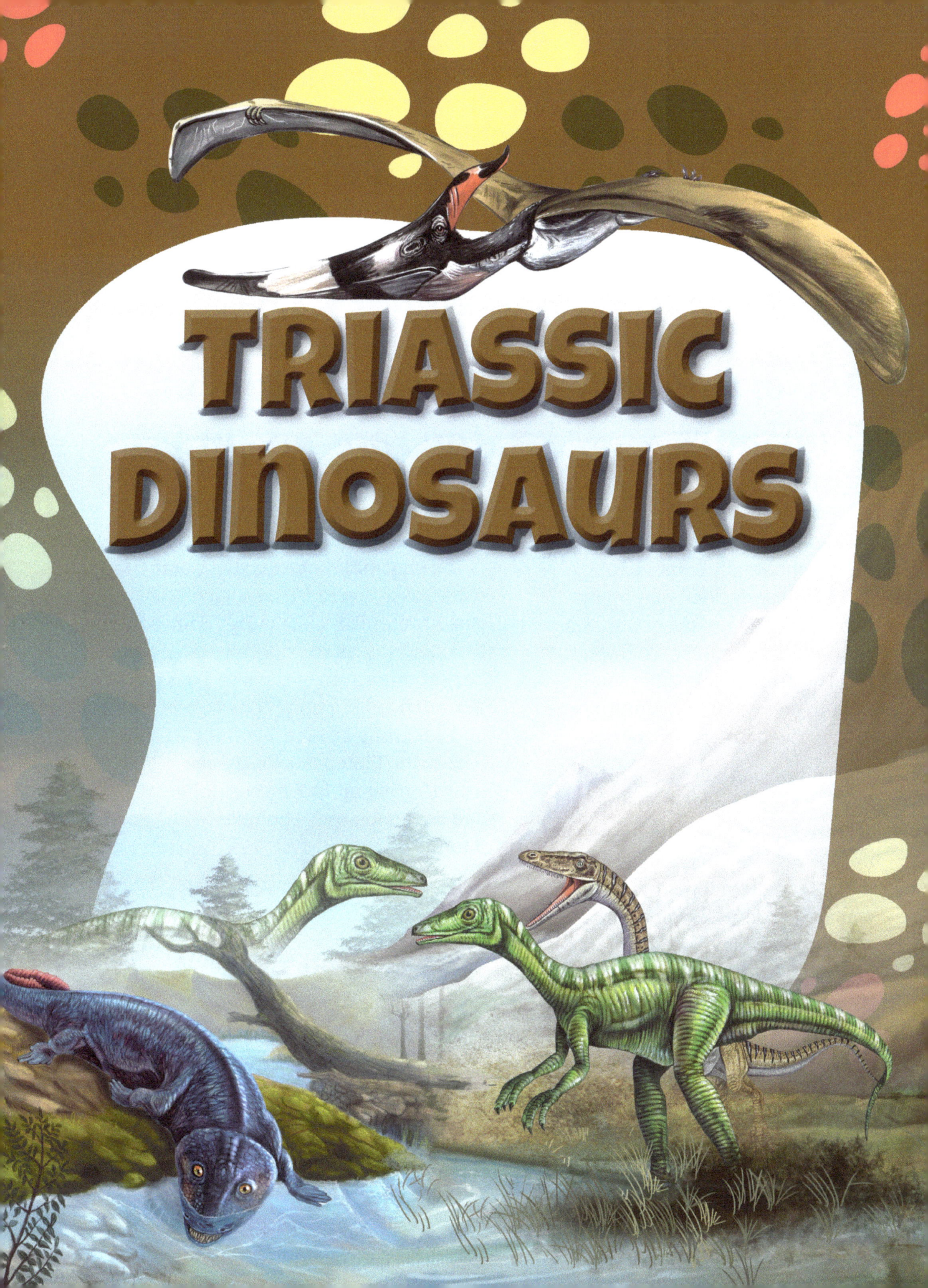

TRIASSIC DINOSAURS

Triassic
Dinosaurs

According to modern dating techniques, the first dinosaurs walked our Earth approximately 225 million years ago during the Triassic period. A diverse group of dinosaurs, varying in size and diet, existed at this time. They were significantly smaller than the gigantic species that emerged in the later Jurassic and Cretaceous periods.

One of the First Dinosaurs

One of the earliest dinosaurs of the Triassic period was Coelophysis, meaning "hollow form," referring to its lightweight bones. Later discoveries revealed that many dinosaurs had hollow bones as a characteristic feature. Coelophysis lived approximately 205 to 210 million years ago in North America during the Late Triassic period.

These dinosaurs were small, slim, flesh-eating bipedal predators with serrated teeth designed for tearing flesh. Fossil evidence suggests they stood up to 3 metres tall and weighed around 27 kilograms, with some reaching a maximum of 45 kilograms. They preyed on smaller reptiles, amphibians, and sometimes even their young. Another early carnivore was Herrerasaurus, meaning "Herrera's lizard," which lived during the Late Triassic period and grew up to 3 metres in length.

The Ancestors of the Famous Jurassic Dinos

Triassic dinosaurs were the ancestors of the enormous species that dominated the Jurassic period. One such dinosaur was Antetonitrus, meaning "Before the thunder." It was considered one of the largest dinosaurs of the late Triassic period, reaching up to 9 metres in length and weighing around 2 tonnes. Another herbivore, Plateosaurus, meaning "flat lizard," grew up to 7 metres long and weighed approximately 3 tonnes.

Coelophysis

The Little Ones
among the Giants

Named after the Roman festival, Saturnalia was a small dinosaur, growing only about 1.3 to 1.7 metres long and weighing roughly 8 to 12 kilograms. Compared to its contemporaries, they were very small, with a very tiny head and long tail. It was bipedal, using its hind legs for movement. An early dinosaur, Eoraptor, meaning "early plunderer," reached about 1 metre in length and lived during the Late Triassic period.

Fossil Studies

The fossil record does not indicate a specific cause for their deaths. Some hypotheses and predictions suggest poisoning or disease, but one of the most plausible theories is a flash flood that may have swept the animals into a depression and buried them rapidly. Support for the theory of immediate burial is derived from the fact that the recovered bones show no evidence of scavenging or weathering.

The Ghost Ranch

In the year 1947, hundreds of skeletons of Coelophysis fossils were discovered in a bone bed at Ghost Ranch Quarry in Rio Arriba County, northern New Mexico. When first unearthed, palaeontologists found no immediate clues regarding the catastrophic event that might have caused this mass burial. The bone bed, a rocky layer, had preserved many fossils, most of them in a complete state, providing an invaluable insight into the lives of early dinosaurs.

Eoraptor

Early Mammals

The early mammals of the Triassic period were very small, reaching only a few inches in length. Many of them were partially arboreal and nocturnal. Most of them were egg-layers, such as Eozostrodon, yet they possessed fur and suckled their young. These mammals were primarily herbivores or insectivores and were difficult to distinguish from the Therapsids and late dinosaurs.

Age of Reptiles

The Triassic period marked the beginning of the Mesozoic Era, which dates back to approximately 251 million years ago. The great extinction occurred following the Permian period. The Mesozoic Era is known as the 'Age of Reptiles'. Only two groups of reptiles were predicted to have survived the Permian Extinction – the Therapsids and the Archosaurs.

Therapsids and Archosaurs

The Therapsids were more mammal-like reptiles, while the Archosaurs were entirely reptilian. During the early Triassic period, it was believed that the Therapsids would dominate the era. However, over time, most of the Therapsids moved towards extinction, while the Archosaurs thrived. In the year 2010, a new species was discovered—Prestosuchus chiniquensis—which measured more than 20 feet (6 metres) in length. An extinct group of Archosaurs, known as the Rauisuchians, were closely related to crocodilians.

Archosaurs

Marine Life

Due to high carbon dioxide levels, 95 per cent of marine genera were wiped out, with very few families surviving the Permian Extinction. Ocean reef-building activity and modern stony corals first developed during the mid-to-late Triassic period.

Ichthyosauria

A group of reptiles known as Ichthyosauria returned to the oceans. By the late Triassic period, these creatures had adapted fully to marine life, developing a streamlined body shape similar to modern dolphins. Their skeletal structure reveals that they exhibited fish-like characteristics, using their tails for propulsion while swimming across the seas. By the mid-Triassic period, Ichthyosauria dominated the marine environment.

Herrera's lizard

Herrerasaurus, also known as 'Herrera's lizard', was one of the earliest dinosaurs to walk the Earth. Around 231 million years ago, Herrerasaurus lived as a carnivore, preying on smaller dinosaurs. These reptiles were the top predators of the Triassic period and actively hunted smaller reptiles. First discovered in 1959, Herrerasaurus measured approximately 20 feet (6 metres) in length and stood 3 feet (1 metre) high at the hip.

Herrerasaurus

Eozostrodon

Eozostrodons were among the first true mammals. They lived during the late Triassic and Jurassic periods, around 210 million years ago. Resembling modern-day shrews, Eozostrodons were approximately 42 inches (107 cm) long. These egg-laying mammals fed their young with milk. They had short legs, pointed snouts, and hairy tails.

Deltatheridium

These early mammals evolved during the late Triassic period. Deltatheridiums were approximately 6 inches (15 cm) long and had exceptionally long tails. They possessed sharp teeth with triangular crowns, adapted for insectivorous diets. Fossils of Deltatheridiums have been found in Mongolia. These mammals scavenged on small reptiles and insects.

Jeholodens

Jeholodens were early mammals with long tails, measuring about 5 inches (13 cm) in length. They were insectivores with highly developed grasping hands. These species were mostly nocturnal and hunted only at night. They scavenged on reptiles and fed on insects.

Jeholodens

Permian Period

The Permian period is also referred to as the 'Great Dying' period, as it followed a mass extinction event. Around 70 per cent of terrestrial species were wiped out, along with 96 per cent of marine life. Scientists estimate that it took nearly 10 million years for biodiversity to recover from this catastrophic event. With climatic changes, cold-blooded reptiles had to adapt to survive in new environmental conditions.

Evolution of Therapsids

Mammal-like reptiles, the Therapsids, developed adaptations to retain body heat and eventually evolved into warm-blooded animals. Therapsids dominated the Permian period, diversifying into various forms, including carnivorous predators and herbivorous plant-eaters. During this period, large reef communities flourished, and bony fish began to populate the seas. The dry climate favoured reptiles, leading to the decline of plant life and water-dependent species.

Pelycosaurs

Pelycosaurs began to evolve with distinct reptilian features. The most well-known Pelycosaurs were Dimetrodons, which had large sail-like structures on their backs. These sails likely played a role in thermoregulation, helping Dimetrodons stabilise their body temperatures during climatic fluctuations. The Permian period marked the final era of the Palaeozoic.

Pelycosaurs

The Beginning

Feathered Theropods

Evidence suggests that birds are a group of theropod dinosaurs that survived the mass extinction at the end of the Cretaceous period. Around 9,000 bird species have evolved from their dinosaur ancestors. Scientists argue that birds are direct descendants of dinosaurs in the same way that humans belong to the class of mammals. More than 100 anatomical similarities between birds and dinosaurs support this evolutionary link.

Plant Life

The Triassic period saw significant advancements in plant evolution. Conifers, including pine trees, appeared alongside ferns, cycads, and horsetail rushes. Triassic plants developed thick, waxy outer layers to prevent dehydration in the hot climate. Unlike modern trees, these plants did not grow to great heights. The tough, fibrous vegetation of this period contributed to the evolution of larger, blunter teeth in herbivorous animals.Triassic oceans were populated with diverse invertebrates. Following the Permian mass extinction, new species evolved, occupying the ecological niches left by extinct organisms.

Amphibians

Although less abundant than reptiles, amphibians were present during the Permian period. The most common Triassic amphibians belonged to the group Labyrinthodonts, meaning 'labyrinth teeth'. These amphibians had flat heads and sharp, conical teeth. They spent most of their time in swampy waters. However, due to their dependence on water, Labyrinthodonts eventually became extinct during the Triassic period. This extinction paved the way for the evolution of other amphibians, including frogs.

Labyrinthodont

In the early Triassic period, the oceans saw many invertebrates, before the massive extinction in the Permian era. Many invertebrates survived the Permian extinction, including clams, snails, scallops and different types of molluscs. The Brachiopods were the most common shelled marine invertebrates.

Brachiopods

Fishes began to evolve, adapting to the aquatic environment. Brachiopods were clam-like species that evolved during the Triassic period. They were a symbol of the "Age of Invertebrates." Brachiopods are often referred to as "lamp shells" due to their curved appearance. The K–T mass extinction was the last major event in which Brachiopods were seen among the vast marine life that disappeared.

Bryozoans

Tiny, seaweed-like colonial organisms known as Bryozoans thrived in deep waters. These aquatic invertebrates, also called 'moss animals', lived in colonies that attached to rocky surfaces, shells, and algae. Some Bryozoan colonies were fan-shaped and ranged in size from a few millimetres to several metres in length. However, the Triassic-Jurassic mass extinction led to the widespread disappearance of Bryozoan colonies from the seabed.

3 mm

The Triassic
Climate

The name 'Triassic' originates from the red and brown sandstone rocks found in Germany. The Triassic climate was interpreted as hot and warm, with a limited number of plant species. There is no evidence of ice caps or glaciers, and the poles were considered to be moist and temperate, making them more suitable for forests. The Triassic climate was extreme, with very hot summers and extremely cold winters.

Reptiles

The animals thriving in this climate had to adapt to both daytime and night-time temperatures, and reptiles outcompeted all other species. Although the climate was very dry, evidence suggests that frequent rainfall occurred, contributing to a more humid environment.

Permian-Triassic Extinction

Around 85 per cent of invertebrate species became extinct at the end of the Permian period. Four-legged vertebrates and plant species suffered significant declines across the Permian-Triassic boundary. Only 30 per cent of terrestrial species survived this period of extinction.

End of the Permian Period

Arthropods

A group of arthropods, called Trilobites, were classified as extinct fossils and were predominantly marine in nature. These arthropods made their last appearance in the Permian period. Several Brachiopod groups, such as Productaceans, Chonetaceans, and Richthofeniaceans, disappeared by the end of the Permian. A group of echinoderms, called Blastoids, which flourished in what is now Indonesia, was last seen at the end of the Permian period. A type of tiny marine invertebrate, called Conodonts, survived the Permian period but became extinct at the end of the Triassic period.

Sea Reptiles

Nothosaurs thrived during the mid-to-late Triassic period and were among the earliest reptiles to rule the seas. Nothosaurs came ashore to lay eggs, similar to modern-day turtles. They had long, narrow snouts with sharp, fang-like teeth. Their lifestyle resembled that of modern sea lions and seals. They could grow up to 11 feet (3.3 metres) in length and were found in large numbers.

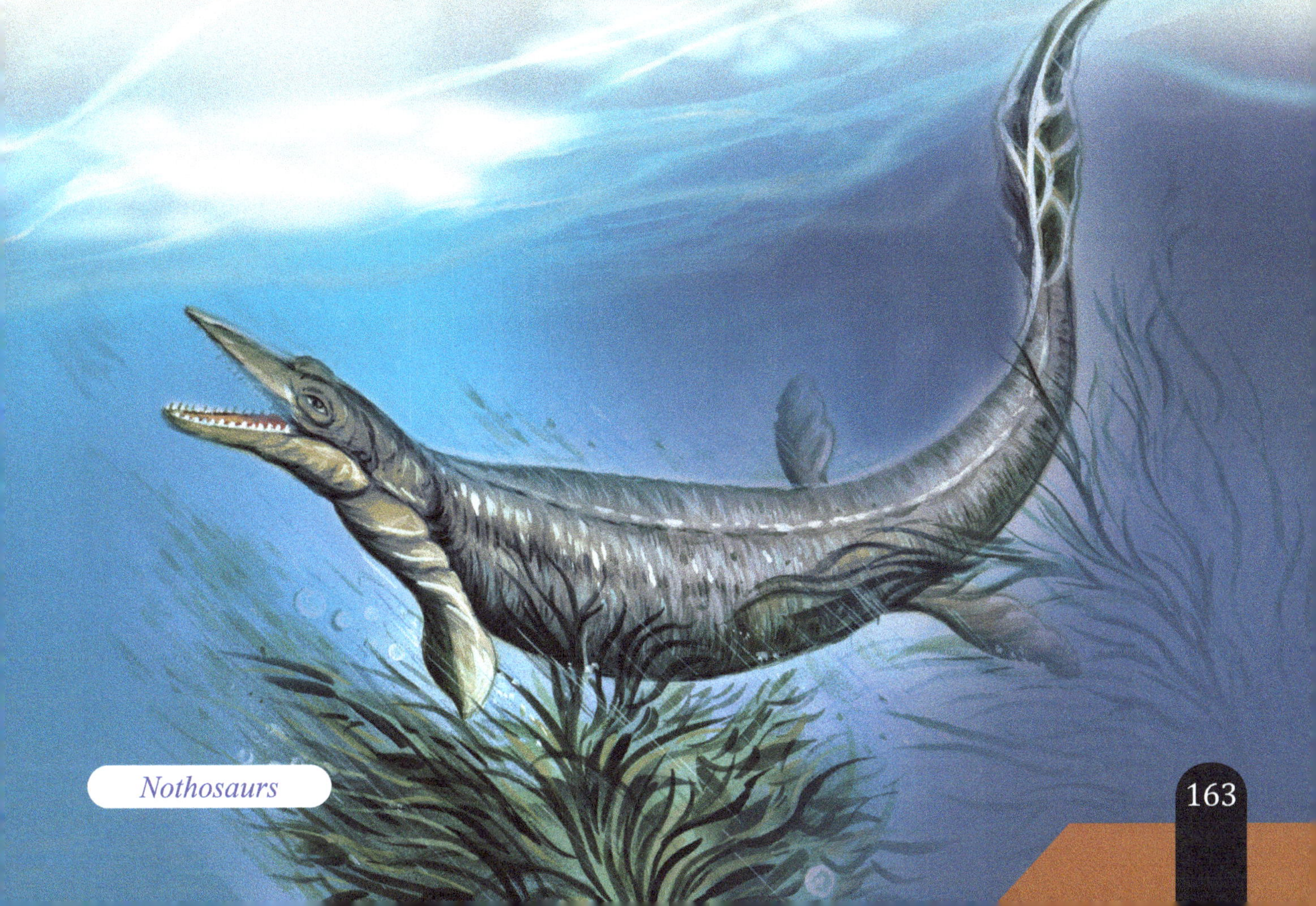

Nothosaurs

Famous Dinosaurs

Pisanosaurus

Pisanosauruses appeared 216 million years ago, during the late Triassic period. They were among the oldest known herbivorous dinosaurs. Interestingly, Pisanosauruses closely resembled carnivores, walking on their two hind legs, yet they were entirely plant-eating dinosaurs. They grew up to 3 feet (1 metre) in length and 1 foot (30 cm) in height. They were fast runners, weighing approximately 15 pounds (6.8 kg).

Coelophysis

Coelophyses were among the first dinosaurs to appear during the late Triassic period. They lived around 200 million years ago and were the descendants of the earliest dinosaurs. The name Coelophysis means "Hollow Form", referring to their hollow bones, a feature rarely seen in other dinosaurs. Thousands of Coelophysis fossils were discovered at Ghost Ranch, making them one of the most important species for studying dinosaur evolution.

Cynognathus

The early Triassic period included Cynognathuses, a group of mammal-like reptiles. Existing around 251 million years ago, they were heavily built animals with wide mouths and sharp teeth. The name Cynognathus means "dog jaw." These creatures had thick coats of fur and gave birth to live young rather than laying eggs. Cynognathuses are considered fascinating ancestors to many modern mammal species.

Cynognathus

Flying Reptiles

The Golden Age

The first Pterosaurs were discovered in a 150-million-year-old fossil layer in Germany. One of the oldest known Pterosaurs, Preondactylus buffarinii, had a wingspan of 18 inches (46 cm) and a very long tail. The 21st century is widely regarded as the "Golden Age of Pterosaur Research."

Pterosaurs

Pterosaurs, meaning "winged lizards", first appeared in the mid-to-late Triassic period. They were the first reptiles to populate the skies. They were characterised by small bodies and long tails. Over time, more advanced Pterosaurs emerged, leading to the rise of Rhamphorhynchoid Pterosaurs, such as Eudimorphodon, Dorygnathus, and Rhamphorhynchus. These flying reptiles persisted into the early Jurassic period. The Rhamphorhynchoid Pterosaurs were eventually replaced by Pterodactyloid Pterosaurs, which had larger wings and shorter tails. These reptiles were capable of gliding over greater distances than earlier Pterosaurs. They also had larger brains compared to the average brain sizes of land and sea dinosaurs.

Terrestrial
Reptiles

Terrestrial reptiles were divided into two major groups: Labyrinthodont amphibians and reptiles. The Cotylosaurs, Therapsids, Eosuchians, Thecodontians, and Protorosaurs were reptilian species that thrived on land. The name Thecodont means "socket-toothed." Towards the end of the Permian period, terrestrial reptiles experienced a dramatic population decline. Around 75 per cent of amphibians and 80 per cent of reptile families were wiped out during the Permian-Triassic extinction. The dinosaurs that survived into the Triassic period had originated during the late Palaeozoic era and gradually evolved into new forms.

Terrestrial Fauna

Tetrapod faunas originated during the Mesozoic era. The Temnospondyls were one of the largest groups of amphibians. They were more commonly found in terrestrial habitats than in aquatic environments, but over time, reptiles dominated these species. Among them, the largest species, Mastodonsauruses, grew up to 13 feet (4 metres) in length. The heavily armoured Aetosaurs, a group of Archosaurs, were among the most commonly found species in the last 30 million years of the late Triassic period.

Mastodonsaurus

Late Triassic
Extinction

Towards the end of the Triassic period, another mass extinction occurred, similar to the one at the end of the Permian. Marine life was nearly wiped out, with only a few surviving dinosaur species. Most aquatic reptiles perished, except for a few Plesiosauruses and Ichthyosauruses. Many large Archosaurs, Labyrinthodonts, Conodonts, and amphibians became extinct. Approximately 20 per cent of all taxonomic families disappeared. It is believed that this extinction event allowed dinosaurs to become the dominant species on Earth.

Ammonoids

The late Triassic extinction severely impacted Ammonoids and Conodonts, two important groups of index fossils in the Triassic rock system. Many Ceratitid Ammonoids went extinct, leaving only Phylloceratid Ammonoids to survive. Many families of Brachiopods, Gastropods, and Bivalves also suffered extinction.

Ammonoids

From Triassic to Jurassic Period

The boundary between the Triassic and Jurassic periods is regarded as one of the most significant extinction events. This event, which occurred 201.3 million years ago, led to the extinction of millions of dinosaur species. Around 35 per cent of marine life disappeared. Except for a few Therapsids and Crocodylomorphs, all Archosaurs vanished. This event happened just before the supercontinent Pangaea began to break apart. Scientists believe that two or three previous mass extinctions contributed to this large-scale destruction, possibly due to volcanic eruptions or climatic changes.

Final Years

In the final 18 million years of the Triassic period, large numbers of reef-building creatures and Cephalopods also disappeared. Interestingly, plant species and other flora were not significantly affected. The Triassic-Jurassic mass extinction is considered one of the largest and most shocking of the five major extinctions during the Phanerozoic Eon.